MAY 1989

DISCARD

Yellow Dogs

YELLOW DOGS

Donald Zochert

THE ATLANTIC MONTHLY PRESS
NEW YORK

Copyright © 1989 by Donald Zochert
All rights reserved. No part of this book may be reproduced in any form or by any electronic or mechanical means including information storage and retrieval systems without permission in writing from the publisher, except by a reviewer, who may quote brief passages in a review.

Excerpt from "Lament" by Edna St. Vincent Millay. From *Collected Poems*, Harper & Row. Copyright © 1921, 1948 by Edna St. Vincent Millay. Reprinted by permission.

Published simultaneously in Canada
Printed in the United States of America

Library of Congress Cataloging-in-Publication Data

Zochert, Donald.
  Yellow dogs.

    I. Title.
PS3576.023Y4 1988   813'.54   88-22353
ISBN 0-87113-254-0

Design by Christine Cansfield-Smith

The Atlantic Monthly Press
19 Union Square West
New York, NY 10003

FIRST PRINTING

For Nancy Ann

Listen, children:
Your father is dead.
From his old coats
I'll make you little jackets;
I'll make you little trousers
From his old pants. . . .
—Edna St. Vincent Millay

1918

1918

I

It was the summer of 1918. The last headers and threshers had come down from the high fields of western Kansas, cutting one final swath through the wheat. Each rig was pulled by six horses abreast. Each was followed by boys and flying hats. The harvest was over.

The sky grew as pure as rare turquoise or jade. At evening streamers of cloud clung to the rim of fading light. The roads were empty. The armies of Wobblies and slackers had straggled north, moving with the harvest.

Larks, not cannon, claimed the countryside around the town of Winchester.

The town itself was dwarfed by the sky. A single street was sufficient for its commerce, quickened in recent months by the construction of an Army training depot fifteen miles to the west. One side of this street was crowded with buildings. Some were frame, most were yellow brick. Flags and bunting hung from their grim facades. A few gray buildings stood opposite, separated by vacant lots. Behind them were piles of coal and the railroad tracks, which ran north and south. The east side of Winchester's main street thus presented a solid front, like a row of soldiers. The other was a line of ruin and weathered timbers into which the sun sank every night.

This was a western town. Wheat fields stretched in every direction around it.

There were few trees. There was little shade. There were only the empty roads and the grain, the grazing fields and the Kansas light. No photographer, sweating beneath his focusing hood, could hope to bridge the gap between that brilliance and the isolated buildings black against the sky. No emulsion could contain that difference.

The Hanson farm lay two miles south of town at the end of a dirt lane off the town road. Here lived Peter Hanson, his wife, Livia, and their two sons, Daniel and Jamie.

Through a fluke, Peter Hanson had been born in France. His parents were in Paris on a holiday when his mother unexpectedly entered labor. They canceled their booking for return passage, postponing the voyage until after Peter's birth. They compounded their foolishness by naming him Pierre; he always went by the name of Peter.

His father was a manufacturer of agricultural implements north of Pittsburgh. The company failed in the 1873 panic. Never having had to face adversity, Hanson met it with a gun at his temple. He felt his wife would wish to accompany him on this final voyage. Theirs had been a happy and successful marriage filled with little luxuries and indulgences. They had been everywhere together: Vienna, Lyons, Port Said. So he killed her too. She preceded him in death by seven minutes.

Peter had no memory of this somewhat melodramatic past, except the kind that recreates itself through endless rumor and expression among relatives and acquaintances. Creditors eroded the estate the old man left. Crooked lawyers carried on the traditions by which the old man had built his success. When everyone had had his fill, only four thousand dollars remained, and this was held in an irrevocable trust until Peter reached twenty-five. The old man had faith in no one, least of all someone named Pierre.

Peter's relatives greeted the dissolution of this estate with pleasure. It justified their own hard lives and penury. Instead of affection they gave him pity, which he did not want. They confused him with his father, something he himself never did. Peter grew up poor, passed along from hand to hand. He worked in mines and factories. He fought the police. Once he thought of going to sea, but never did—preferring earth to water. The day after he received his inheritance, he was on his way west to farm. He knew himself, and measured all things by what he left behind.

He built a house on a slight rise in the prairie called South Hill. The barn and its feed lot stood behind the house, with a stony path leading down to pasture. It was flanked by low and clumsy outbuildings. The surrounding fields were planted, surprisingly, to stunted corn. This made the Hanson farm something of an island in a sea of wheat and grazing land. Peter Hanson farmed corn and a little barley, raised chickens for the town market, had kept milk cows—all well west of the meridian beyond which such things were said to be possible. The farm was not large, but was more than enough for one man. Or one man and one woman. Without the strong back and willing heart of his oldest son, Daniel, it would have been impossible.

No matter what the land gave him—wind and dust and hail and withering heat, as well as blinding storms and snow—Peter Hanson kept one thing in mind. He was a long way from Pittsburgh, the coal mines, the factories, and Paris, France.

Several buggies stood unattended at the head of the lane. Their patient bays and chestnuts, some still in harness, cast quivering black shadows on the ground. The midafternoon air was still.

Jamie Hanson lay on his stomach beneath the bed of an elegant buggy, playing the most innocent of games: war. His legs and feet extended into the bright sunlight. The toes of his boots dug into the dry earth. He held his head motionless. His forehead was smudged with dirt where he had brushed the hair away, the better to see the enemy. His eyes were narrowed to slits against the afternoon light, which seemed to well up like a geyser from the distant sky.

Before him was the empty lane. Beyond that was a golden patchwork of fields, bristle, thimblegrass.

In another age a boy in this shadowy cave beneath the buggy of Mrs. Millie Curtis might have imagined himself secure, peering safely out at the defiant light. But Jamie Hanson had been born at the wrong time. The peaceable fields that stretched before him now, winding like calico to the horizon, were filled with imaginary Huns. The Boches. The barbaric, square-jawed soldiers he had seen in magazines, who every moment crept closer through the trembling stalks of corn.

Jamie inched forward.

His round face was nearly flush with the spokes of the buggy wheel. His legs slithered into the shadow. His cheek rested lightly against the stock of a rifle he had shaved from a piece of soft pine a few days earlier. He squinted down the barrel, following the empty lane to the point at which it met the road from town.

Slowly, he squeezed the trigger.

"Pa-chew!"

"Pa-chew!"

"Pa-chew!"

He whispered off several rounds. The terrible Huns fell one by one, whirling like dervishes in the fields and on the dusty lane.

They lay dead without bleeding.

Jamie pulled the rifle back from between the spokes. He rolled out from under the buggy, scrambled to his feet, and raced across the yard of yellow grass in one graceful motion. He had watched John Curtis, the neighbor boy, practice this before John enlisted, and he loved John Curtis as much as he loved his own brother Daniel.

"Pa-chew!"

"Pa-chew!"

The Germans were shooting back.

Jamie stumbled, turned a somersault in the dirt, and was on his way without stopping. He threw himself into the protective cover of verbena at the corner of the yard. After a moment he sat up.

Sweat trickled from his face.

At eleven, he had lost the traces of childhood, save for his soft round cheeks and his small mouth—always pursed, as though waiting for a kiss. His forehead was broad, like all the Hansons'. His brown eyes, full of sudden emotion—sometimes bewildered, sometimes insolent—were the eyes of a boy passing unawares into adolescence. They searched the corners of the house for a sign of movement.

The house seemed deserted. It was wrapped in silence. A screened porch extended along the front of the house and part way around the side. Green vines with small red flowers climbed on trellises next to the screen, blocking summer light and heat.

Jamie studied the patterns of shadow.

He was on his feet again. He dashed across the yard with the rifle gripped tightly in one hand, passing directly beneath the empty flagpole from the porch. He rounded the far corner of the house and flattened himself against the clapboard. His breath came in gasps. His eyes scanned the horizon.

The voices of his mother's friends drifted through the parlor screen over his head.

"Why did they do it?"

"I believe he didn't subscribe to the bonds."

"Was he badly hurt?"

"Only his pride. He was badly frightened, I should imagine. He signed a check for fifty dollars."

"Fifty dollars!"

"Old Mr. Hofer did the same thing," another voice declared. "But he stopped payment the next morning."

"It's hard times."

"They're plainly different. Miles and I have very little truck with them."

There was a general murmur of agreement.

Livia Hanson's friends were sitting in the darkened parlor,

as they did every Tuesday afternoon. They were making bandages.

"Have you heard from John," someone asked.

Jamie snapped to attention.

"We're all so *proud* of John," someone else added.

"Yes," Millie Curtis said. "We *have* heard."

The rifle dropped from Jamie's hand. John Curtis was Daniel's best friend, and Mrs. Curtis was like another mother, to both Hanson boys. Jamie looked at the window. By stretching he could just barely reach the sill. He jumped for it, grabbed onto the ledge and pulled himself up.

The women were seated on the far side of the parlor near the porch door, for the air. Bandages were spread out on their laps and stacked in a neat pile on the hassock between them.

Millie Curtis was holding a letter in one hand and putting on her eyeglasses with the other.

" 'Just a few lines to bid you folks farewell,' " she said. She peered about the room over her glasses. " 'We are in Brooklyn as you can see.' " She continued:

> "By the time you receive this we shall be on the ocean. I am prevented from giving you the name of our ship or declaring our destination but when you write use the address above. Be sure to spell out American, Ma, as there is an Australian Expeditionary Force as well. For the rest of it, E.F. is okay. There is no cause for worry—"

Millie Curtis put the letter down. "I'm sorry. Did you want to hear this?"

A murmur of assent.

"I just assume, because he's my John. . . ." Millie lifted the letter from her lap. She continued:

> "There is no cause for worry. Uncle Sam has taught us all a few tricks we didn't know before. The worst was homesickness but that has passed. We got here safe as you can see.

There was a review the other night, our last in camp. It was a grand sight. Colonel Lewis, you often read of him in the newspaper, is our regimental commander. It was sure fine to see the three battalions in line with the band in front and then as they swung into step every man alike in step and in line and the band of fifty pieces playing a grand old march which is said to be one of the best in the army. Ma, it beats anything you ever saw. There was quite a fight in the Red Triangle Club that night but I didn't get hurt, don't worry.

"We drilled pretty steady and except for being pretty sleepy I feel like a spring chicken most of the time. We arrived here two days ago and were instructed in gas defense work but this is my first chance to write. Gosh, it's awful stuff. There are two kinds—one like an onion only considerable worse. Most of the boys had streaks running down their cheeks when they came out but you just can't beat that American grin can you? I always wanted to see New York but didn't see much, just Lady Liberty. I made pals with a fellow from Alabama as I believe I told you in my last. He's a wild one, all red hair and freckles. He wants to know all about Carrie but I ain't told him much. I'm still looking out for Danny. Tell Danny hallo will you and I will write to him from the other side. I haven't heard from him yet but there's a war on as they say. I am sending some of my baggage back so check the express in town."

Jamie looked at his fingers. They were turning white.

" 'It's a hard thing to tear yourself apart from home and the bosoms of your loved ones,' " Millie Curtis read.

"I do think of you all at night, innocent Carrie and Bud and Pa and you, Ma. Well somebody's got to do it right? It's sure a grand flag so please don't worry on my account. We'll all be soldiers before this war is over. As you can tell from my letter I'm in good cheer and there is no cause for alarm. Do you have a ladies company yet, I seen several here.

"You can write to the address I gave. I never did get Carrie's letter that you mentioned she must of broke her arm. But it will catch up with me I'm sure. Give her a kiss from me and make her blush will you? Here's a handshake for Pa and a kick in the pants for Bud. He'd be here if he could I know it. Well I suppose I'll close. It's raining here today but I'll bet a nickel the sun is shining in Kansas. It's the grandest place on earth. The boy from Alabama is named Harold Lester Holmes but he answers to Tiger and I guess it fits. I'm going to write to his Ma for him on account of his hand being broke at the Red Triangle. Well, Ma, farewell I guess. Don't worry about me. This time last year I was working the south field with Bud and Pa and Dan. Your soldier son, John."

The ladies sighed. The room filled with an uncomfortable silence. Just before he slipped to the ground, Jamie saw Mrs. Curtis touch a hankie to her eye.

"Then yesterday came this printed card," he heard her say. " 'The ship on which I sailed has arrived overseas.' It's signed by John."

"So he's over there," someone said.

"And what of Daniel," someone else asked.

Livia Hanson's voice was thick. "He went to town yesterday and registered as a soldier, on account of his twenty-first birthday falling on Sunday."

"Oh! There's another fine boy, Livia!"

"I should say," Millie Curtis agreed.

"We have so much to be proud of."

Jamie secured the grounds around the house. The road to town was still empty. Now and then he crept out into the fields, hoping to lure the Krauts into the open. They refused to take the bait. He circled the house two or three times but drew no fire.

The drowsy heat rose from the fields.

Crouching near the cellar door at the rear of the house, Jamie tried to fathom the silence of the German guns. They could be gathering for an attack. They could be having an early supper.

His nose flared, alert for the scent of onions. His makeshift rifle swept back and forth along the line of the horizon, and finally came to rest pointed directly at the open door of the barn. Inside was darkness.

It was the first time he had thought about the barn.

He moved swiftly across the yard to the henhouse. Light shimmered in waves from the tin roof of the adjoining crib. Jamie squeezed between the two buildings, looked both ways for picket troops, and dashed toward the barn. He had learned about pickets from Mr. Solomon McKenzie, who was ninety-two years old.

Jamie knelt on one knee at the open door. All he could hear was Old Don, munching oats in his stall. The boy's face tightened into a knot of indecision.

If the Huns were inside the barn, surely they would post a sentry to watch the door. On the other hand, they could all be busy eating. Or perhaps examining Old Don, whose back was misshapen from too many years of hard work, first in the mines of western Pennsylvania, then in the fields of western Kansas.

Jamie's fingers ran nervously along the barrel of his gun.

In a moment he realized what he would have to do: cross the open doorway, work his way along the side of the barn through the feedlot, and reach the back door of the barn without being seen. He backed up cautiously two or three steps and held his rifle in front of his body with both hands, like John Curtis had shown him.

Then he made a dash for it.

At the very center of the open doorway he threw himself forward, somersaulted on the cinders, and was safely on the other side.

The Huns never saw him.

Quickly, he moved along the side of the barn. At the back corner he stopped, extended the rifle beyond the edge of the building and moved it slowly up and down—hoping to draw enemy fire.

There was no sound.

This was one of the hard things about war, not being sure where the enemy was lurking. Jamie tensed. From far out in the fields came the brief slurry of a lark's call. There seemed to be a high and awful silence in the air. He drew the rifle in against his chest, to steady his nerves and give himself courage. He could feel his heartbeat through the wooden stock.

"Well," he said to himself in a voice so small no one could possibly have heard it. "Farewell, I guess—"

He leaped out from behind the building and landed on both feet in the blinding light.

Jamie's mouth opened in surprise.

His eyes grew wide.

Directly before him, hanging from the splintered branch of an ancient peach tree, was the body of a yellow dog. The creature was bound to the tree by its hind paws. Its front legs hung stiffly downward, and its head dangled off to one side at an awkward and unnatural angle. Its throat had been slit.

The dog's dark eyes stared at the earth. In the scant grass beneath the tree was a circle of blood.

2

Livia Hanson kept the gauzy curtains pinned back from the two parlor windows yet always drew the shades to within ten inches of the sill. They glowed like golden barriers against the light. They fluttered sometimes in the breeze, as though waves of insubstantial light were beating up from the flat fields of Kansas and breaking softly against the house on South Hill.

Inside, even on the brightest day, the Hanson parlor was dark and restful, a refuge from ordinary cares. The drawn shades suited Livia's notion of what it meant to make a home: a balance between the needs of her family and the reality of the world outside.

A tall white bookcase in one corner held Livia's handy set of encyclopedias with their worn maroon bindings and translucent pages, the novels she loved to read, and a few volumes of poetry in blue and gold. Daniel's geology books were stacked sideways on the bottom shelf. In another corner of the room, behind Peter's chair, a small pine chest held Jamie's lacquered blocks, a slouch hat, a book about caravans in Egypt, a piece of lustrous chalcedony that Daniel had found and given him for good luck. These were the toys of a boy who played alone. Livia's chair, across from the sofa, was covered with delicate handwork.

Here she often sat to sew, to read, and to make bandages for the Red Cross with the ladies of the neighborhood on Tuesday afternoons. Peter Hanson's chair was large and functional. He was its only adornment.

He sat with a newspaper spread carelessly across his lap. A few sheets had slipped to the gray carpet.

Jamie stood penitently before him.

From the sofa Daniel could see the back of his brother's head, his brother's nervous hands, and nothing more.

"You saw no one," Peter asked.

Jamie shook his head. "I was all over playing Krauts, halfway down to John's and back, and there wasn't no one around. And when I got to behind the barn, next to the cow yard, it was just hanging there in that old peach tree—"

"You know the dog?"

"Never seen it."

"What kind is it?"

"Cur."

The boy's hands fidgeted behind his neck. He stared at the carpet. He felt as though he had done something gravely wrong but wasn't sure what it was.

Peter looked across the room at Daniel. Their eyes met for a moment, then Daniel looked away. Daniel turned his book face down on the sofa, stood up quickly, and walked toward the door. He paused a moment to look at his father, but said nothing.

The screen door banged shut as he stepped onto the porch.

"The poor creature, who never harmed no one," Jamie burst out. "Who would *do* such a thing, Pa?"

The boy finally mustered the courage to look his father in the eye and saw his mother in the doorway between the parlor and the dining room. Livia wore a plain apron over her cotton dress. She had been in the kitchen preparing supper, but was brought to the parlor by the sound of their low voices, the slamming of the porch door, and a certain palpitation about her heart.

She wiped her hands on a towel so as not to soil her apron. "Who would do *what* such a thing," she asked.

There was no immediate answer. The yellow shades fluttered softly.

"Peter?"

"Boy found a dog hanging from that old tree back of the barn, Liv. The one that don't bear fruit."

Livia's fingers reached for her throat.

"Yellow dog, with its throat slit. Strung up by its hinders and left to die."

Peter stared at the window across the parlor. A moment earlier he had seen Daniel pass by on his way to the barn. Now all that showed beneath the shade was a blaze of white and empty light where his son had been.

"Daniel's taking care of it," he said at last.

Father and son had worked together a long time. A shrug of the shoulder, a smile, a glance, an unsolicited hand: In labor and these mute gestures they were bound together as closely as they were by blood.

When Daniel smiled, his face gained a lively radiance people loved him for. At those times his brown eyes sparkled with something of Livia Hanson's high-strung force of character. He was coveted by other boys' mothers, who saw all the sad inadequacies of their own sons and were blind to those in Daniel. Their sons wanted to leave the home place for fast cities and fast money. Daniel didn't. Something about the home place and the life the parents had made dragged behind all his dreams like an anchor and brought them back to their starting point. Three summers in a row he passed up the chance to continue to college at Emporia. As each summer drew to a close, he saw the labor that was left to be done at South Hill and stayed. In this, he kept his own counsel. Whether for honor or pretense of honor—and who can read the motives of character in a young man?—Daniel had never let anyone down.

Peter saw this much in his son: He was steadfast. The two were not at all the same, but as Daniel grew older, they proceeded in parallel paths that yet converged. Father, son. It would be too little to say that Peter loved him. It was as though he had created a new line of the family, mending the gap left by his own father. More often than not, he marveled at his son.

Daniel worked quickly in the far corner of the yard behind the house, trenching a shallow pit in the soft earth. The yellow dog lay off to one side.

When he had squared the corners of the hole and smoothed the bottom, he slid the blade of his shovel beneath the dog and lowered the burden gently into the ground. He scraped loose gravel over the creature's body and tamped the tiny grave several times with his boot, feeling the earth yield. By the time he was finished, the back of his shirt was soaked through with sweat.

He carried a shovelful to sprinkle on the ground beneath the tree, covering the dark stains of blood. Then he replaced the shovel to the barn. He walked slowly back to the corner of the yard, where the dog's grave lay as smooth as a scar.

The wind was rising. At the horizon thin streamers of cloud had begun to appear. The harvested fields spread out before him. Far away in France boys his age were huddled in dark trenches, heads down, with only the faint glow of a cigarette to tell that they were alive. At Soissons, at Faverolles, in Meuniere Wood, armies of men faced fear and bravery side by side. Daniel stood there a moment before the rising wind and Kansas fields, with his hands shoved deeply into the pockets of his overalls.

Then he turned abruptly and strode toward the house.

The dining room was silent as Daniel took his place across from his brother. Livia sat at the end of the table closest to the kitchen. Her hands were folded in her lap. She seemed to be studying every ligament and vein. Peter sat gravely at the head of the table.

"I believe you will find the Bible next to your mother's side of the bed," he declared. Jamie slid off his seat without a word and left. After the boy returned with the book, it took Peter several moments to find the passage he sought. His finger pressed hard against the page as he read:

" 'Think not that I am come to send peace on earth. I come not to send peace, but a sword. For I am come to set a man at variance against his—' Well! Let's see here!"

He fell silent. His finger followed the verse.

" '—at variance against his father,' " Livia said deliberately. " 'And the daughter against her mother. And a man's foes shall be they of his own household.' "

Peter frowned. As he closed the cover of the Bible, a small puff of dust ascended into the air.

"It's food for thought, at any rate."

Daniel looked up for the first time. He reached across the table for the cream.

Livia's voice broke sharply. "You're not going to discuss it with your father?"

Daniel turned toward his father.

"When I went into town yesterday, I registered for an exemption."

"So I surmise," Peter said.

"As being opposed to war on the grounds of conscience."

"As I well surmise."

"I *knew* it," Livia cried out.

Jamie looked quickly from his parents and back to Daniel. The remainder of the meal passed in silence. Daniel ate quickly, and he carried his plate to the kitchen when he had finished. The screen door banged behind him as he left the house.

"I'll catch him," Peter said, pushing his chair back from the table. But Livia didn't answer. She didn't look up. The food on her plate was untouched.

A short time later Daniel walked alone along the back lane, toward the Curtis farm a mile to the south. The sun was just setting. The sky was turning a pale gold, and the green of the barley fields had deepened to verdigris. The air held an unexpected hint of coolness.

Daniel's closeness to the Curtis family went beyond the usual harbor from rough waters that one family will provide for the son of another—making no demands, enjoying him for what he is and not what they wish him to be. They embraced him with affection and considered him one of their own. Of course, Old Man Curtis bossed Daniel around as surely as he did his own two sons. And Bud, the older of the Curtis boys, was a sour and disagreeable man whose own dreams had long since been dissolved by the hard Kansas summers and the claims of his father. But the warmth of the other members of the family was generous and open. Even the old man, who thought rather grandly of himself, had taken Daniel aside one day after watching him work the hayrack with John, and had spoken very mysteriously about the extent of his wheat fields and the vigor of his cattle and the possibility that some day Daniel would in some way be part of it. Then he had put his arm around Daniel and squeezed the boy's shoulders.

"We been on this land since the time of the buffalo," the old man liked to say. "We ain't new, like some folks I know. We ain't green. We're part of it, from the day it come up from the sea."

Millie Curtis was younger than the old man but several years older than Daniel's own mother. She was, in an odd way, more motherly. Daniel never heard her complain. She never cried, as Livia had so often and so helplessly the summer after Jamie was born. Even when she was fretful, cheerfulness was always breaking in. If she had any hysterical weaknesses, Daniel did not know them. He knew only her warm heart and pleasant face.

John Curtis was much like her: happy, accommodating, warmhearted. He had been Daniel's friend for as long as Daniel could remember. They were one year apart, but so alike they counted themselves as brothers. If it seemed at times as though they were taking different paths, they were inevitably drawn back together by their common lodestone of memories. Bud Curtis was another story, a brother to no one. Nearly thirty, he was thin, dark, quick-tempered, and crippled in the right leg ever since a threshing accident when he was still on the green side of twenty. He was a dog, chained to a stake beneath the Kansas sky. Bud's passion was horses. At one time he had hoped to set up in New York State or Florida as a breeder and trainer of racehorses. His father opposed him. One day the old man took Bud aside. "We been on this land since the time of the buffalo. There is Curtises go back to the time of Coronado. My grandpappy was part Indian. His grandpappy was all Indian. We ain't new. We ain't green. And goddamn it, boy, we ain't easterners." Then he spoke mysteriously about the extent of his wheat fields and the vigor of his cattle.

There was one other Curtis, the reason Daniel turned up the lane in the twilight. John was gone, but his sister, Carrie, was not. She was nineteen, and very comforting in her conversation.

Daniel stopped halfway up the lane, near the second gate. Across the pasture was a small pen. Inside this was a beautiful bay pony, its coat glistening in the thin light. Bud Curtis stood with his back to the lane, holding the broken handle of a hay rake out before him. He moved cautiously from side to side. A bridle and blanket lay on the ground in the corner of the pen.

Daniel opened the gate, slipped through, and closed it behind him. He was about to go on quietly up toward the house when he changed his mind and headed down into the pasture, taking long strides as he came off the lane.

"Breakin' her?" he called out. "Two men are better than one!"

A sparrow flew up from the grass at Daniel's feet. The pony held its head high, shaking its mane. Its eyes were filled with fright.

"Don't see but one man here," Bud Curtis called back. He didn't turn. He was stripped to the waist, and his skin glistened with sweat. His back rippled with cords of muscle as he lifted the rake handle into the air and brought it down squarely on the filly's head. The beast shuddered, and backed heavily into the corner of the pen. Bud took a sharp breath and swung the handle sideways, catching the pony on the side of the neck. Then he spun around on his bad leg to face Daniel.

"This here's a slackin' beast! Don't want to be ridden!"

"You'll kill it."

"Might be right." Bud's mouth was as thin as a boning knife. He brought the handle against the side of the pen with a resounding smack. "There's a fence between you and me from here on out, Danny. Don't try to cross it!"

Bud's breathing came hard; it was clear that he had been at his task since long before Daniel arrived. The horse cowered behind him, a feather of dark blood trickling into its eye.

Daniel stared at him a moment, then turned on his heels and headed back up the slope toward the house.

"Last time you'll be prancing up *that* path!" Bud called after him.

The big house was quiet. It was twice as large as the Hanson's. An aged cottonwood shaded it from the sun and gave it a cool, tranquil air even on the hottest days. Daniel walked quietly around to the back and glanced up at the kitchen window, where Millie Curtis's face hovered silently behind the screen. Their eyes caught in a kind of surprise, and Daniel stopped. Millie came close to the screen. There was a heaviness in her face and in her voice.

"She's gone on down to the creek, Dan."

"I surmised."

Millie spoke softly. "Bud's out front with the horses. He's mighty dark...."

Daniel found Carrie sitting on the fender of an abandoned binder down by the dry creek. She wore her plain blue-striped dress. She glanced back over her shoulder when she heard his footsteps.

"I figured you would come, Daniel."

"I feel a need of you."

"I feel a need of *you*, Daniel."

He sat down beside her. She gave him a smile mixed with bittersweet and placed her hand in his. With her other hand she smoothed her dress. Daniel stared at his boots.

For a moment neither spoke.

There had always been this silence between them, a mute familiar sea in which the currents of their thoughts met and blended without ever coming to the surface. They had played together as children—snap the whip and Indian chief. They had worked the harvest and spring planting, had roughnecked and wrestled. They had grown up. They had grown even closer since John had gone away. Now, when Daniel looked into Carrie's gray November eyes, he saw something far different from the past they shared, or the past they shared with John. He saw something wider than Kansas, as deep and mysterious as the future. Until this moment, their conversation from their shared silence had gone everywhere but to the point.

"Do you think it takes courage?"

"I don't know. I guess so. But it's not for showing courage."

"What are your reasons?"

"It's wrong, is all."

"But you *got* to have reasons."

"That's my reason. It's wrong, is all."

"Daniel?"

"Yes."

"We sure done a lot together, you and me."

"Well, we have, haven't we?"

"Bud told us at supper."

"Bud did?"

"It's all over town, and half the county, is what Bud says. Says you're nothing but a slacker that's afraid to fight. A yellow dog, and all. With John off fighting—it's hard. Ma don't believe it. She just don't believe it of you. And Pa was mighty dark. He went off to town in his motorcar to talk with Sheriff Bonner. But I figured you would come, just as always."

"Bonner tried to talk me out of it, on the grounds of duty."

"Sheriff Bonner did?"

"He's on that registration board along with Mr. Bull Hadley and Doc Pratt. They all three tried to talk me down from it. Said it was dead wrong not to go, and they even brought up John as well, being the first to enlist and all. But it's my right, ain't it? To make my own mind up on it?"

"What'd you tell them?"

Daniel shrugged. "My conscience won't permit it, that's all. Killing's wrong."

"Dan?"

"Yes?"

"You know what Ma said?"

"No."

"'Conscience just ain't practical. Not in this day and age.'"

"Maybe not. I'm the one that's got to bear it, though. No one else. Except you, if you feel . . ."

Carrie was silent a long time. The darkness of the fields was rising around them.

"Danny?"

"Yes?"

"Ma loves you very much, Danny."

Carrie turned her head away and looked off into the fields.

"It hurt her very much," she added softly.

"I'm sorry."

"But you know what?"

She turned her head and looked at Daniel. Her eyes were filled with tears.

"No."

"I knew you were going to do it. I just knew. I knew you were going to do it ever since John went off. I knew you were going to do it. I just *knew* it. I knew . . ."

Daniel put his arm around Carrie's waist and drew her toward him. They talked together for a long time and fell silent and talked again, circling each other through that sea of silence, drawing nearer and nearer to their true feelings. They talked long after the sound of the motorcar came across the fields from the town road to the west. They talked long after the sound of angry words drifted toward them from the house. Their own voices were soft and gentle in the rising darkness.

"It's just like going off to war, Carrie. That's the way I see it. A different war, that's all. One way or another I'd have to go."

"Are you afraid?"

"No more than John. I guess I can stand up to it."

Now and then, from far out on the dark acres, a breeze carried the tiny cries of the poorwills toward them.

"Daniel?"

"Yes?"

"I am being forbidden to see you. Pa said at supper I am not to see you any more."

"Your ma knows I'm here."

"I know."

"So does Bud."

"He does?"

Beyond the fields, and above them, was a silent vault of darkness, and in the darkness were a billion stars.

"I never told it to anyone, Carrie. I love you."

"Me, too," Carrie said quickly. "I love you, Daniel."
He walked home in darkness, alone, beneath the Kansas sky.

Peter and Livia Hanson lay side by side in the dark bedroom. Their bodies did not touch. The room smelled stale, as though it were reserved for sickness and the weak exhalations of sleep. Peter was speaking quietly:

"Don't know much about being a father. Never had a father to call my own. But I know about working. I know about working hard. I know about standing on your own two feet and not letting yourself be bossed around by any man, no matter who he is. That's what I tried to teach 'em, Liv. Be your own man."

"You know about the grace of God, Peter."

"Don't know much about it."

"You called for the Bible at supper."

"Don't know much about it at all. I seen the grace of God at work around here. It's got its goddamn nose stuck high in the air."

"Peter!"

"It's got nothing to do with it, Liv. Old Man Curtis has the grace of God. And four thousand acres of damn good wheat. That makes a combination you can bet on. But look at that God-forsaken poor excuse of a bastard son he's got. Bud's a cripple in body, and I don't hold that against him, because it wasn't his doing. But he's a cripple in spirit too. Who made him that way? The old man. It wasn't the accident. Men handled worse odds than that. It was the old man. And the grace of God."

"What about John? He enlisted right up. He volunteered, first in the county."

"Just why do you suppose, Liv?"

"He's a . . . good boy—"

"He ain't no boy. He's a year up on Daniel."

Livia was silent. "He believes in his country," she finally said. "He answered his country's call. . . ."

Peter sighed. He threw his arms back, and his hands banged loudly against the headboard.

"You're right. He's a good boy. He's a damned fine boy. But he volunteered to get away from Curtis, Liv. He saw what happened to his own brother, didn't he? He volunteered to get away from someone else running his whole life for him."

"So he joined the United States Army?"

"I said he's a damned fine boy, Liv. I didn't remark on his brains."

"Peter! It's our *own* son—"

"I was raised up by nobody, Liv. Aunts and uncles I hardly knew, and a schoolteacher outside to Pittsburgh, Pennsylvania. I lived in other people's houses all my life. That's all I got to go on. This country will give any man a chance, long as he's man enough to stand on his own two feet and not buckle under. Take a look at me. I got myself into a few scrapes along the way, standing up for what I believed was right—"

"You've sure bragged enough about that before the boys."

"I wasn't bragging, Liv. It's best they know what it's like. It ain't no storybook story. Whatever I got, I worked for. And *you* worked for, just as hard. That's the American way. I stood up to get it, and I didn't back down once. That's the American way too. You seen what we did to this place, just land and sky and whatever a man can make out of it. You and me did it, Liv. You and me and Danny, when he come of age. There's no way they can take away what we made out of this with our own sweat and work, standing up to everything. This here's our *country*, Liv, and our *place!* This *here!*"

Peter slammed the palm of his hand down hard on the bed between them. "Dan's a good boy too, Liv," he said. "Don't forget it. There's a sense we couldn't have done it without him. Looking back, I'm glad to have him. I'm *proud* to have him. He got raised pretty good, thanks to you, and a lot of folks around this county think the same way. He studies them geological books. He thinks for himself and always has. He's a hardworking boy and he gives a care for others. That's the important thing—he gives a care for others. That counts for something, don't it? Try and say that about Bud Curtis. Try and say that about the old man. That boy's a whole lot like me, when it comes down to it—"

"He *is* like you."

"That's what I say. There comes a time, you gotta let go of the reins. Just slap him on the hindquarters and say, 'Okay, boy, it's your race after all. Run it. Show 'em what you can do!' It ain't easy, Liv, I'll agree. But you gotta turn 'em loose to stand on their own."

"He won't even *talk* to you about it, Peter. He doesn't talk to us about *anything.*"

"He *did* talk about it, Liv. Caught him down to the barn, on his way over to Carrie Curtis."

Livia was silent a moment.

"What's his . . . reason?"

"Said he's been thinking about it ever since the call for volunteers went off. That it's wrong killing, every way he looks at it, and his conscience stays against it."

"His conscience is all?"

"Says it's on his shoulders, nobody else's, to stand up for what he feels is right."

A silence began to grow between them.

"What did you tell him, Peter?"

"I told him we stand behind him, Liv."

Livia Hanson suddenly twisted around in the bed as though she were in the grip of a convulsion. Her arms and back trembled. She turned her face toward the pillow.

"Oh, Peter! I'm so *ashamed!*"

3

Bull Hadley drummed his fingers on the top of his huge walnut desk. He clenched a cigar between his teeth and squinted toward the front of the narrow store. His eyes were small and dark, the same color as the desk.

Fans whirred softly overhead.

Bull Hadley operated the only general store in Winchester, drawing business from many miles around. He was the county clerk. He served as chairman of the Liberty Bond Drive. He was vice-chairman of the Winchester Businessmen's Association. Last year he was chairman; next year he would be chairman again. He was a delegate to the Businessmen's Association of Kansas, and once had a drink with Charles Sumner Pomeroy of the United States Senate. He had friends in high places.

The store was on the "good" side of Winchester's main street, the side from which large storefront flags hung in patriotic splendor in the late morning air. Hadley's desk, at the rear of the store, nearly blocked the small hallway that led back to the musty stockroom and the loading dock. The aroma of spices and fresh linens and feed mingled with the scent of Hadley's cigar and the faint cold odor of ashes from the wood stove.

Hadley rarely left his desk. It was the roost from which he surveyed the world.

"We had woodcocks in Missouri," the widow Murphy said

from the front of the store. "The husband was fond of woodcock. My Lord, everywhere you stepped they'd fly up from your feet. And come spring they boomed so to keep the devil himself awake. Drumming and booming, just like you sitting back there in the dark, Harry. We'd go out to the woodlot, the husband and me—"

"I'm busy," Hadley said.

The widow Murphy turned her back on him. She leaned against the cash register near the front door, watching the automobiles and horse-drawn wagons pass the window. After the first flurry of morning business she had tidied every bin, barrel, counter, and shelf in the store. Everything was neat, except for Hadley's desk. No one was allowed to touch Bull Hadley's desk except Bull Hadley. He imposed his own order on it.

The top of the desk was strewn with invoices. Three law books were stacked carelessly on sweepings of dust balls and tobacco crumbs. A cardboard box filled with packets of plug tobacco balanced atop a disorderly mound of torn and twice-folded catalogs. A sepia photograph of Bull Hadley's daughter was propped between the law books and the plug tobacco. She looked wistfully at him, his only daughter. She had been a Sunflower Girl. She had helped with the dishes and gone to church. She went to school in Emporia and learned how to be a globe-circling newspaper woman. Then she moved to Chicago and went to work for the *Inter-Ocean*. She never wrote home.

On the left side, corners perfectly aligned with the edges of the desk, was a small sealed manila envelope. On top of the newspaper open on the desk was an ashtray, a momento of Bull Hadley's most recent trip to Kansas City, on which he had obtained the contract for supplying the new Army training camp west of town. In one fell swoop the contract had doubled Hadley's income. It had given him something to spread around to the officers who had "assisted" him in his bid, as well as an ample excuse to celebrate. He drank three of them under the table the night the contract was signed, two colonels and a major, and then did the town up right with the commander of the camp—careening across the cobblestones with two women they knew only as Elsie and Ivy. "Black as the night," he told the boys at home. "And twice as bad." He found the ashtray in his suitcase when he unpacked, a reminder of good times and good friends. The naked figure of a sea nymph reclined in a large pink seashell. The nymph's hands were folded behind her head. Her glazed face stared up at him without a flicker of emotion. Her legs extended over the edge of the shell, and her tiny ceramic feet helped brace it on the desk.

Bull Hadley placed his black cigar carefully between the open legs of the nymph. From behind he could hear the high, piglike grunts of Emmett Minor on the loading dock outside, throwing heavy sacks of meal onto the wagon.

The sergeant's uniform was pressed and spotless. His tie was tucked neatly into his shirt. His face was round and red. He stepped inside the door and stopped, peering toward the darkness in back. Then he strode briskly down the aisle.

Bull Hadley reached for his cigar.

"You're late."

"Sorry, Mr. Hadley. There's a war on. Is the wagon loaded?"

"I should think so, seeing as we arranged for you to be here fifteen minutes ago. You realize this is a place of business. Occasionally we have customers wander in?"

The sergeant glanced down at the envelope on the corner of the desk. Then he looked around to see that the store was empty except for the widow Murphy, who still leaned against the cash register with her back to them. Hadley stuck the cigar into his mouth and stared toward the front of the store as the sergeant picked up the envelope, balanced it lightly on his fingertips, and slipped it into his pocket.

"I'll give your regards to the commandant."

"You do that. And I'd be obliged at a little more punctuality."

The sergeant turned and looked toward the plate-glass front. The window was a blaze of light.

"It *is* a great day for a parade, isn't it," he asked.

"The parade's tomorrow."

"That's what I mean. Any day's a great day for a parade in these times. It gives a boost to the spirit—see that flag coming down the street. Makes everyone mighty proud."

"I can guarantee it'll start on time," Hadley said.

He spit a piece of tobacco off his tongue. Then he swiveled in his chair and called for Emmett Minor.

Minor appeared quickly in the stockroom doorway. He was a scrawny youth, stripped to the waist. His hair was long and tangled. His chest was covered with sweat and fine white dust. His expression was doleful, like that of a dog who's misbehaved.

"You done with that wagon?"

"Yes, sir. But that meal's bad."

"How's that?" Hadley snapped.

"Meal's bad, sir. I split one of the bags by accident. There's grub worms all through it."

Bull Hadley's eyes narrowed. He pushed himself to his feet and gave the sergeant a sickly, apologetic smile. "You'll excuse me," he said. He turned abruptly, grabbed Emmett by the arm, and almost carried the boy back into the stockroom. He pushed him against the wall.

"Who's that I'm talking to?"

"Sergeant Gibbons," the boy stammered. His eyes were terror-stricken.

"You simpleminded sonofabitch!" Hadley cracked the lad across the face with his open hand. The boy slid slowly down the wall, settling on the seat of his pants. His fingers reached for his mouth as Hadley bent toward him. "You know better than to say something like that in front of the sergeant," he hissed. "There's no worm in that meal. You understand?"

Emmett Minor stared at the floor.

"I say, you understand?" Hadley drew his hand back.

The boy shook his head. He didn't look up.

Hadley turned on his heel and reentered the store. The sergeant stood with his back to the stockroom, hands folded behind his back. He rocked gently back and forth as he studied the delicate plaster tracery around the edge of the high ceiling.

"War *is* hell," he said softly.

Hadley sat down heavily at his desk. He opened the bottom drawer, withdrew two crisp twenty dollar bills from the cashbox, and placed them on the corner of his desk. He pushed himself to his feet again.

"The boy's simpleminded. Don't pay no attention to him, sergeant. I took him off the street, just like a stray dog. Tried to make something out of him. But he wouldn't know a grub worm if he saw one. I checked that meal. It's fine. Finest meal in the county, I guarantee it."

The sergeant rocked back and forth, still looking at the ceiling. "Little grub worm now and then never hurt anyone," he said.

"The wagon's loaded," Hadley said. "I don't know what you're loafing around for, wasting the taxpayer's money. Try to be here on time next week, sergeant. With you running the Army we'd lose this war for sure."

Bull Hadley stalked toward the front of the store. The sergeant picked up the twenties, slipped them into his shirt, and left through the storeroom. He cast a contemptuous glance at Emmett Minor as he passed.

"Does it hurt," Livia asked.

"No."

"You still need a mother, nevertheless."

She sat on the kitchen stool. Her cotton dress covered her ankles. She held Daniel's hand in her lap, palm upturned, and pricked gingerly at the sliver in his finger with her sewing needle.

"My goodness, I held this same hand the first day you went to town school. Do you recall? After that, you went alone. Such a hand! A helping hand! Do you recall when you broke your arm?"

"Of course I recall."

"And do you recollect what Doc Pratt said to me?"

"No."

" 'Hold his hand, Mother. It'll heal twice as fast and twice as strong.' "

She looked at Daniel with a hesitant smile. There were dark sleepless smudges under her eyes. Her hair was drawn back severely from her face.

Daniel looked beyond her, out the kitchen window.

Livia lifted his hand from her lap and patted it gently. "When you were just a baby, Daniel, I'd put my finger in your palm—one finger is all that would fit—and you'd close those little fingers around it. You had the smallest fingers! The smallest I'd ever seen! Now look at you. A man's hand! It feels—different."

"Can you still read palms?"

"Don't be foolish," Livia said. But she quickly reconsidered. "Of course I can, though I haven't since you were younger than Jamie." She gazed at his palm. "Yes, the line of heart is deep and clear. See here where it commences, very high on the hand? That signifies happiness—and pride. Perhaps too much pride." She kept herself from looking up at him. "Here you can see, fate joins your heart. It does not merely cease or cross the line of heart, but joins it. All your ambitions will be gratified through your affections, Daniel. The line of sun is lacking. Also lacking is the hepatica. That's a good sign. The line of head—can you see here, where it curves ever so slightly downward? A tendency toward Bohemianism, Daniel. Imagine! You a Bohemian! And can you see, the line of life commences here, at the line of head—signifying that intelligence and reason are your guides to conduct. Your line of life is forked down here at the end. That signifies many things, perhaps that your life shall end in a place far removed from where it began—"

She caught herself. Daniel stared at his hand.

"Have you written to John Curtis?"

"Haven't had occasion to," Daniel answered.

"John's been gone a long time. Concluded all his training and now he's over there. In France."

"So I hear."

"Don't you think you should write him? Why don't you write him today? I'm sure he'd appreciate a kind word from home. Especially from you, Daniel."

"Don't know what I'd tell him."

"You could tell him about . . . home," Livia insisted. "He's a long piece from home."

She fell silent.

"Why do you suppose John rushed so to sign up?" she said suddenly.

"He knew I wasn't going to."

"He *knew?*"

Livia resumed digging in Daniel's finger with the needle.

"We talked about it off and on before he went. I told him the way I was thinking, and I believe he felt pretty much the same. He was in a different boat, is all."

"In what manner?"

"Being bossed up and down the county by his old man. Being bullied around by that brother of his. In some folks' eyes he was always second to me. I'm not being heady. That's just the way it was. Joining up gave him a chance to prove himself better. He decided as soon as I declared myself against it."

"You never mentioned anything about this. We never knew you had these thoughts in your head, about a furlough and all. You never discussed it with your father. Fact is, you don't tell us much of anything, Daniel."

"I do, if you listen."

Livia sighed. She held the needle firmly between her thumb and forefinger, and tried to keep her eyes focused on the vibrating tip.

"Who were you obliged to see in town?"

"The board is Mr. Hadley and Doc Pratt and Sheriff Bonner."

"Well, it's just like you, Daniel, to seek a furlough. Your father surely needs you. Hold still. It's hard running a farm. There's the home front to consider too. Soldiers have to eat. The more crops that are grown, the more soldiers can be sent to fight."

She smiled. The sliver had come out.

"Doc Pratt made that suggestion to me, that I put in for farm work. He was pretty kindly about it, I'll have to say. He declared everybody goes who's able, is the rule, excepting the overly religious. And even they can petition for the farm as being in the interests of the war."

"You mean . . . you didn't take a furlough when offered?"

"I couldn't. I sought exemption on the grounds of conscience, as being opposed to the war in its entirety. Now it's up to them."

"In what manner?"

"There's no grounds for conscience in the law, is what they said. Only for those as don't wear buttons and things of that sort. Like old Mr. Hofer refuses to wear buttons or get a motorcar on account of religion, even though he's got the money for it. His boys are the same. Mr. Bull Hadley said to think it over good and give it due consideration. He declared they had the power to commend me into jail or direct into the Army if I don't agree to serve."

"Jail?"

"Accused me of being on a high horse and being too stubborn to get on down."

Livia looked at him intently.

"We always had the highest hopes for you, Daniel."

"Hopes don't enter in. I love this country as much as the next fellow and better than most. That's what I told the board. It just comes down to killing's wrong and so is war."

"Right and wrong, Daniel—they're like—they're things no one really knows. What I mean is, they're things people differ on—"

"Is killing right?"

"Well, no. Not in most cases."

Daniel stood up suddenly, towering over her. "You see? It's something a person has to decide for himself. That's what makes it a free country. Is it wrong to stand up for what's right?"

"I don't know."

"Is conscience a crime?"

Livia was silent. Daniel stepped past her to the window, where he could look out at the barn and the fields and the tiny yellow scar in the corner of the yard.

"We put all our hopes in you, Daniel," his mother finally said. "We gave you all the love in the world. We never thought you'd be the one to break our hearts."

"Old Man Curtis says Carrie's not to see me anymore."

Livia twisted in her seat.

"Carrie?"

There was no answer.

Peter made his way to town in late morning, going directly to Hoover's market in order to deliver his eggs to Kate Hoover. She paid him in silence, then busied herself rearranging a crate of lettuce that looked to be in perfect order. Her husband, Jim Hoover, had disappeared through the curtains in the back of the store as soon as Peter stepped in. When Peter drove Old Don up the street to the depot, his reception was no warmer. He usually passed a few minutes each day in conversation with William O. Waters, the station agent. But as he descended from the wagon, William O. Waters drew down the metal shutter on the ticket window.

Peter turned his back on the depot, tied up Old Don, and crossed the empty street to the sheriff's office, where he found Abel Bonner engaged in a game of Napoleon with Little Harry, Bull Hadley's wayward son.

The sheriff was short and muscular. Now middle-aged, he had drifted down from the prairies of South Dakota shortly after the turn of the century. As an outsider he was called upon to adjudicate a dispute between farmers and ranchers in the neighborhood of Winchester, and so impressed the parties to the dispute with his evenhandedness that he was soon put forward as a candidate for sheriff. He had kept the peace ever since.

Little Harry was his contrary in almost every regard. He moved slowly, in thought as well as body. In his mid-twenties, he was so large that his clothes had to be special-ordered from Kansas City. His straw hair was never combed. His thin blond eyebrows were almost nonexistent. The narrow set of his eyes, and their porcine nature, gave such a plain clue to his character that many residents of town—especially women and girls—deliberately crossed out into the street to avoid confronting him.

He had already been exempted from service on the grounds of his weight, and consequent inability to run more than fifty yards without complete loss of breath. The fact that his father once had a drink with Charles Sumner Pomeroy of the United States Senate had nothing to do with it. In truth, of all the people in Winchester who disliked Little Harry, none disliked him more than Bull Hadley himself. Hadley kicked the boy out of his house as soon as his wife died, sending him to live in a room above Frank Sacco's barbershop. Hadley paid the rent to be rid of him. Little Harry swept up for Sacco, helped out Simon Turner as a pallbearer, and did other odd jobs. The single window in his desolate room overlooked his father's store. He spent long hours there, dreaming of the day when he would be vice-chairman of the Winchester Businessmen's Association.

That the sheriff actually played California Jack and Boathouse Rummy and Napoleon with Little Harry was a measure of Abel Bonner's ability to keep the peace. No one was ever long out of his sight.

Little Harry stared sullenly at the cards. He absentmindedly drummed the fingers of his free hand on the table. Just as Sheriff Bonner bid a wellington, further confusing the boy, the door flew open. Peter Hanson stepped into the small anteroom.

The brilliant light from the street outside surged around him. He didn't move from the doorway.

"I'll have a word with you, Bonner."

"Come in."

Peter looked at Little Harry.

"Outside," he said.

Bonner had already put his cards face down on the table and pushed back his chair.

"I figured you'd be in, Pete. The boy was just mentioning something about a dog out at your place."

"I'll take care of it myself, if need be. I'm coming to you first."

"Probably a warning," Little Harry said. "As for them who put themselves above their country. I heard it's a yellow dog. . . ." He smiled and showed his broken teeth.

Bonner rose abruptly from his chair and walked toward Peter. "We'd best have the privacy of the street," he said, taking Peter by the arm. The two men stepped out onto the wooden sidewalk. Bonner reached back and closed the door. Shortly, Little Harry's face appeared in the window.

"I got a high regard for you, Pete," Bonner said, when Peter had finished telling him about the incident of the previous afternoon. "I got a high regard for that boy of yours. But he's making a grave mistake."

"He's doing what he feels is right. We back him, his mother and me."

"Still a grave mistake. He's been offered a farm furlough. That comes out of respect for you, Pete. But he declined. Feelings run high on a thing like that."

The muscles in Peter's jaw worked in and out. He stepped down from the sidewalk into the street.

"We known each other a long time," the sheriff said. "You're a good man, and I'm not afraid to declare it. That's why I got to tell you this: Don't try to fight his fight, Pete. That's the worst thing you can do. He's going down a hard road. But that's the biggest fool mistake you can make—Pete? Pete?"

Peter turned and stalked across the street. The sun had now fully illuminated the huge flags and bunting that hung from the storefronts behind him. He untied Old Don and drove down the street to Hadley's store.

Bull Hadley himself was about to emerge as Peter opened the door.

"Just the man I want to see," Peter said, blocking the passage. His voice was suddenly hoarse. He looked up and down the street to see who was watching, but the street was empty.

Hadley ran a finger around the inside of his collar. "I'm going to dinner, Hanson. I'm busy."

"You're always busy. My boy Dan was in to see you the other day, Hadley. Declared his—"

"Don't have time for official business. Step aside."

Peter didn't budge.

Hadley's round face began to turn crimson. He drew a large bandanna from his pocket and mopped his brow.

"This is not the time or place to be discussing official business," he repeated. "I'm a storekeeper. I'm out to lunch. You want to discuss that son of yours, you will have to make an appointment for the entire board. We are doing our duty, which is more than can be said of some. Now, will you kindly step aside?"

Peter stepped back and Hadley came through the doorway into the full sun. He held the bandanna clenched tightly in his fist as he turned and began to walk down the street.

"Trouble for him means trouble for you," Peter called after him. "I can provide it. Now or later."

Hadley stopped. He slowly turned around. There was just the faint trace of a smile on his livid face.

"I already sent a message out to your place, Hanson."

"I received it."

"You don't know what you're saying. If I were you, I'd consider your remarks. This here country's got a war on. I left orders for a messenger to go out to your place today from camp. The board will deliver its finding tomorrow and that boy of yours is required to be there. There's nothing to keep him from serving his country, Hanson. He's a sound boy, he's fit, he's of age, and he doesn't have a leg to stand on."

Hadley mopped his face again and stuffed the handkerchief back into his pocket.

"I'll give you a damn good piece of advice, Hanson. Make a soldier out of that boy between now and then."

With that Bull Hadley turned his back and headed down the street toward Lane's saloon.

Two hours later Old Don was still standing patiently in front of Jack Hurley's saloon at the south end of Winchester's main street. Flies buzzed around his misshapen back. His blond tail swished back and forth. He was blind—too many hard years in the Monongahela mines. His head was down. Now and then his ears twitched. His black nostrils were flared wide, as though he sensed some kind of danger.

The saloon's swinging doors were hooked open, to allow more air. Inside was a cool cavern of darkness. Peter Hanson sat alone at the bar, near the door. His feet rested lightly on the rung of the stool. A frosty stein of cold beer sat before him, half consumed. Near the rear of the saloon three men huddled together at a small table. One was Simon Turner, the mortician, whose establishment was directly across the street from Hurley's. All three were well along the way to being drunk, even though it was only a little past midday. They laughed, and began to sing softly, in raspy voices:

> *Hush, little Thrift stamp,*
> *Don't you cry.*
> *You'll be a War Bond*
> *By and by.*

Jack Hurley, an old friend of Peter's, stood alone behind the bar at the rear of the room. His arms were folded solemnly across his chest. His hands were tucked into his bloused sleeves. He watched the door.

"More cars than horses today," he said.

The men in back agreed. "Horses are for them as don't care to come into the twentieth century," one of them said. "Shirkers and slackers, might as well say. Amishmen and Mennonites. Might as well say corn farmers—"

"Them automobiles don't shit in the street, either," one of his companions added.

Peter stared at his reflection in the mirror over the bar. He noticed the flush on his face, the strength of his neck, the husky bulk of his shoulders. He saw Simon Turner rise unsteadily to his feet and stumble toward him, from the back corner of the saloon.

Peter turned calmly to face him.

The mortician's eyes were bleary. There was a pencil-thin mustache across his upper lip, and he needed a shave. His delicate nose was pitted, and his lips were drawn back from his teeth.

"You tell him, Simon!" someone said from the back of the saloon.

Turner put his face up to Peter's.

"You always been a scrapper, Hanson. How'd that boy of yours turn out so goddamn yellow?"

Jack Hurley took two quick steps forward, but he wasn't quick enough. Peter's fist flashed across the front of his body and crashed into the mortician's face with a sickening crunch. Simon Turner's eyes wobbled and rolled backward. He hit the floor hard. A trickle of blood began to work its way down into his mustache.

Chairs scraped in the back, but it was Jack Hurley who leaped around the end of the bar and took Peter by the arm, pulling him toward the open door.

"You hadn't ought to have done that, Pete. He didn't mean nothing. By God, I saw it coming. I should have stopped him. You'd best be getting on home. Come on now, Pete. . . ."

He guided Peter gently to the sidewalk.

On the way south from town Peter stood upright on the buckboard. He held the reins so tightly in his fist that his knuckles turned white. His mouth was open, and he drank in air in great gulps. He had a fine view of the countryside—the green and golden distances, the azure sky, the hard brilliant light, the air of stillness and repose.

His eyes scanned the horizon, warily.

Jamie Hanson slithered forward on his stomach into the shadow of the verbena. The grass smelled burnt, as though it had been struck by phosphorus. Closing his eyes and turning toward the sun, he could see the rocket's red glare.

His face was covered with sweat and dirt. He pulled his mother's wicker picnic basket along behind him. When he was safely behind the verbena, secure from enemy fire, he opened the basket. He withdrew several sheets of white cloth torn into strips, a pair of scissors, a bottle of liniment, a bottle of rubbing alcohol from the barn, a small vial of iodine, and his father's roll of good white tape.

He spread all of these out neatly in the grass.

"Lie still, soldier. Don't move," he whispered to himself. "Will you have a drink of water from my canteen?" He peered at the roots of the verbena, conjuring up a face. "Is it you, John? Is it you, John Curtis? Don't move! Lie still! Easy now, boy. Does it hurt? Does it hurt a lot?"

Jamie wiped his brow with his sleeve and turned his face away.

"Looks bad to me," he said to himself. "Looks real bad to me."

Jamie failed to hear the faint put-put-put of a motorcycle turning off the town road. A soldier in uniform steered a straight line up the very center of the lane between the cornfields. A feather of white dust floated into the air behind his machine.

By the time the soldier was halfway to the house, the noise was too loud to ignore. Jamie sat up. The soldier stopped his machine at the edge of the lawn, swung one long leg over the seat, punched down the kickstand with his boot, and walked over to the verbena. His face was long and tanned. His brown eyes sparkled. Behind him the bright chrome of the motorcycle's handlebars caught the sun.

"Medical corps," the soldier asked grimly. Then he smiled. Jamie was speechless. He had never been so close to a soldier.

Suddenly the rider snapped to attention. He brought his hand up smartly in a salute—but whether to the corpsman under the verbena or to the American flag that now fluttered from the pole over the porch, it was impossible to say.

"Good work, son," the soldier said. "You can't be Daniel Hanson?"

Jamie sprang to his feet. He turned and dashed toward the side of the house. "Daniel," he called. "A soldier's here! A soldier!"

A moment later Daniel walked around the side of the house, wiping his hands on an old rag. As he passed the corner, he heard the parlor door open, and knew that Livia had stepped out onto the porch.

"You're Daniel Hanson," the soldier asked.

"Yes, I am."

The soldier reached into his blouse and withdrew a small pale envelope. "You're required to appear before the registration board at ten thirty tomorrow morning. This here constitutes your official notification, on the orders of the board, and has the force of law."

The soldier had delivered this speech before. He handed the envelope to Daniel, looked into his eyes a moment—and saluted. Jamie, at Daniel's side, saluted back.

The soldier turned, mounted his motorcycle, and headed down the lane. Daniel watched him through the dust. Just as the motorcycle reached the town road, it swerved and seemed to disappear. Old Don and the wagon turned into the lane, the horse coming up the rise at a trot.

"Look at Pa!" Jamie said. "Pa's standing up for the soldier!"

4

Peter Hanson drove the wagon to the back of the house without stopping. Jamie went flying after him. When he reached the barn, Peter reined in Old Don and jumped down from the buckboard. "Let him loose. Water him," he snapped. He stalked into the house and slammed the door behind him.

"There's a silence coming between us," Livia warned at supper. No one answered.

"I'm going to the parade tomorrow," Jamie said a little later. "It's Loan Day." No one spoke. "Could you be a soldier, Pa? If you wanted to," Jamie asked.

"What happened to your hand, Peter?"

"Caused a Hun to cease to be," Jamie answered for him.

That night a soft breeze sprang up from the south. The breeze rustled in the corn. It whispered in the stubbled wheat fields around Winchester. Lights from isolated farmhouses glimmered like beacons on a dark sea, drifting apart. Great streams and eddies of Kansas stars hung in the inky darkness overhead. They seemed near enough to touch. To the north of town the Mennonites said their prayers and went to bed. Their kitchens smelled of cabbage. The men were lean and hard and muscular; the women, plain, with dark, doelike eyes that now and then burst into a kind of glorious flame. They were yoked to patience and to innocence. No one knew them very well. No one had much to do with them. Far to the west of town on the prairie artificial arc lamps burned throughout the night at the Army training post. The sound of artillery fire drifted northward on the wind. Boys who had been to France talked quietly with boys who had never been away from Kansas. "Of course you're afraid. Don't say you're not. Every mother's son is afraid. When I was in France . . ."

Winchester itself was wrapped in silence.

Sam Briggs had supper at Lane's saloon, next to the print shop. The print shop used to be a newspaper office as well, but the newspaper had failed. Sam cleared his throat over and over until he caught the eye of Miss Mary Cole. "A very pleasant evening," he said. "Made much more pleasant by your presence." Miss Mary Cole smiled. She had rose-petal lips. Next door, James Kent's photographic studio was closed. Kent was gone from town to visit his mother. The mortician's establishment was dark. Simon Turner was across the street at Jack Hurley's saloon, very drunk and very apologetic to one and all. "Pardon me, I didn't mean it," he told everyone. "Could you be bothered to buy me a drink?" Frank Sacco sat on a stool in front of his barbershop, next to the mortuary. He stared across the street at the small vertical space between Hurley's saloon and the burned-out building adjacent. To Sacco's eye the space between the two structures seemed filled with fireflies; they were western stars. Hadley's store was closed. Guy Martini, the cabinetmaker, sat on the floor in the rear of his cabinet shop next door. A single electric light burned overhead. He held a bottle in one hand, and with the other gently stroked the side of a rosewood highboy as though it were a woman's thigh. He felt soft, sensuous vibrations through his fingertips.

In the small apartment to the rear of his music studio Mr. Frisco Fritz opened an ornate Chinese cabinet and withdrew a small piece of resin wrapped in cloth. He closed the cabinet door quickly, because it also contained a thin blue volume of poems by Heinrich Heine. Lovingly, he applied the dark resin to the bow of his violin. Frisco Fritz was not his real name. Frisco Fritz was what he called himself when he came to Winchester from San Francisco seven years earlier and set up as a music teacher. His real name was Oskar Frank. Only his mother, in Jena, could have said so. And for all he knew, she was dead. Frisco Fritz was bad enough. Fritz was what the Heinies were called. Consequently, Frisco had contributed more to the Liberty Loan than any other resident of Winchester had—two hundred and ten dollars.

He lifted the violin to his chin. The dark wood gleamed. Frisco's eyes darted to the windows. They were closed. The room was very hot. He began to play, certain that no one could hear him. Just to be sure, his thin lips formed the words silently:

*Ich weiss nicht was soll es bedeuten,
dass ich so traurig bin....*

James and Kate Hoover's produce market was closed. They were at home, where James was finishing up the last of the supper dishes and setting them out to dry. Langer, the bootmaker, had been gone two months. He'd said he was going to Texas, but no one had heard from him. His shop, next to the market, was dark and dusty. No lights burned in Joseph Webb's harness shop and garage, next door. Webb was down at Jack Hurley's. Sheriff Abel Bonner sat on the wooden bench in front of the sheriff's office. Dr. Homer Pratt sat next to him. Their legs stretched out before them on the sidewalk. They were looking across the street at the depot, where a single light shone inside.

"I've known him all his life," Doc Pratt said softly. "I've known Pete and Livia just as long. He's a fine boy. A very fine boy."

"So's John Curtis," Sheriff Bonner said.

"Yup. You're right."

"One goes, the other don't."

"I'm just a country doctor. I'm not a philosopher."

They waited for the sound of the evening train in the darkness, coming from somewhere, going to somewhere else.

At South Hill, Peter and Livia sat at opposite ends of the front porch. The soft breeze made the leaves tremble on the vines climbing the trellis. The old house creaked and groaned, as though it were sinking deeper and deeper into the darkness. Jamie was asleep upstairs, dreaming of soldiers on motorcycles.

Peter and Livia had hardly spoken a word to each other all evening.

"Where's Daniel gone to," Livia asked.

"Gone for a walk, down the town road."

"I don't know how I can face them, Peter. How can I face Millie Curtis, whose own son has gone off to war?"

"Stand up and face them, that's all. We stand behind him."

They lapsed into silence.

Now and then Peter lifted his hand from the cold water in the white basin illumined by light from the parlor window. The hand was still swollen. He moved the fingers slowly, and made a fist.

"We're his family, Liv. We're all he's got."

"Us and his conscience."

A mile away Old Man Curtis and his wife sat far apart on the west porch of the big Curtis home. They looked out past the cottonwood in the dark. Across the fields from the west came the mournful song of the evening train, fading and growing stronger. Bud Curtis was a slim shadow in the corner of the porch. He sat on the floor with his back against the wall. The brim of his hat was pulled low over his eyes.

Old Man Curtis stood up from the swing and walked to the screen door. He was in the middle of a blow. "The sheriff don't like it either," he declared. "There's a provision in the law for those as appeal to Scriptures. There's a provision in the law for those as consider themselves already a part of the kingdom of the Lord. They can serve as doctors on the battlefields. They can build bridges and lay down roads and load supplies on them big ships that cross the ocean. They can work on farms, providing food. Do you understand the law, woman? Do you know what the law is? The law is the law. There ain't no provision in the law for slackers and cowards."

"For yellow dogs," Bud Curtis said.

"There ain't no provision in the law for those as don't want to follow the flag of their own country," the old man said. "Now you take the Curtises, Millie—my grandpappy and his grandpappy and his grandpappy before him, so I assume. We been in this country a good, long time. We ain't never shirked. We took what we could get, and then we took a little more. You and me, woman, we got our own flesh and blood off as a soldier. Doing his duty in the trenches. Through mud and dark, rain and storm."

"And French ladies," Bud Curtis said.

"You ain't up to going, Bud. So keep quiet," the old man counseled. "But John's off showing that kaiser what the spirit of American boys is all about. That's a brave boy that answered his country's call. Just as you'd have done, Bud, if you could. We got every right to be proud of him. We got every right to have no truck with folks as don't have the courage to do the same. Is that plainly understood? I don't want no dealing with them. I don't want Carrie seeing that boy. I don't want you seeing that Hanson woman. I don't want no dealing with Peter Hanson. You know something, Millie? I never did like that man. I put up with him on account of those boys of his. Real cocky sonofabitch. An easterner, too. Do I make myself plainly understood by all?"

"Ought to be burned out," Bud Curtis said.

"I ain't saying that," the old man corrected him. "I'm saying this here's a free country, and we can do as we damn well like."

Millie Curtis sat in a white wicker chair off to one side of the porch. She stared at her husband's back.

"You're mighty silent, Ma," the old man said after a time. "Here I been doing all the talking. What are you thinking?"

He received no answer.

"Ma?" he repeated.

Millie's voice was soft and low. "It's funny, Miles. I do believe that's the first time you ever asked my opinion of me."

"Say what you're thinking."

"I think we loved Daniel a long time. I think we ought to go on loving him."

Old Man Curtis stiffened. He began to rock back and forth on his heels, peering out through the screen at the extent of his wheat fields and pondering the vigor of his cattle.

"Do forgive me for asking," he said sourly.

He hitched up his trousers, nudged open the porch door with his boot, and let loose a stream of tobacco juice into the flower bed next to the steps.

"I don't believe that boy," he added, almost as an afterthought.

"You don't believe Daniel?"

"He told me once this country here was raised up out of the sea," the old man said. "Millions of years ago, before the time of the buffalo. I don't believe that boy knows what he's talking about."

"I recall a rock he showed me, a lime rock with seashells in it," Millie said.

The old man thought about it. He shook his head. "He don't know what he's doing, that's all. Don't know what the hell he's doing. Too young to know." There was a trace of sadness in his voice.

Silence came up from the fields. The night seemed to hold nothing but stars and silence, and distant points of light drifting away from each other in the darkness.

At long last, Old Man Curtis said, "Where's Carrie gone to?"

"Gone for a walk, up the town road," Millie said sweetly.

She was standing next to the abandoned corncrib off the town road, just as she had said she would be.

"You're a girl of your word," Daniel said, coming down through the tall grass toward her.

"I always been, Danny."

"Your pa know you're here?"

"He's busy fuming."

"Your ma know?"

"Deep down she does. But she ain't saying. I can tell in her eyes, though. She knows how I feel." Carrie paused a moment. "It's on my shoulders, as I heard someone say."

They faced each other hesitantly in the darkness.

"We'd best get away from the road, in case an automobile comes on down from town," Daniel said. He led her around to the opposite side of the crib and opened the door. "I recall when we came here as kids, and old John got himself stuck headfirst down the side in the corn," he added.

Carrie laughed. "That's like him, ain't it?"

She sat on the earthen floor in one corner. Daniel sat across from her. The shed was so small they could almost touch. Through the open slats they could see the stars of the Kansas night.

"I miss him," Carrie said suddenly.

"Me too."

"Hope he ain't gone away for good."

"He'll be back."

"He brung us together in a way, him and you being such close pals. Almost like two brothers. More so than Bud, I would say."

"Well," Daniel said.

"You couldn't hardly avoid me, hanging around."

"Who says I wanted to?"

Carrie didn't answer.

"I remember the time *you* were on my shoulders."

"Well, that hardly takes a memory! Fourth of July, last year. You just sweep me off my feet, Daniel Hanson!"

"Everybody sure buzzed."

"I guess I can stand the talking. And maybe add a little to it!"

"Shouldn't care, anyway," Daniel said.

"That's right. Do what your heart tells you, Ma always says."

"Your ma never did."

"Maybe so. You never know. She might have." Then she asked, "What's your favorite thing."

"Next to you, I suppose?"

"Of course, next to me." She was serious.

Daniel thought a minute. "This here land, I guess. South Hill and all that goes with it. It's hard to put words to it. There's a lot of things."

"You don't like chocolate anymore?"

Daniel suddenly laughed. She wasn't serious after all. "Chocolate's my favorite," he agreed. "Next to you, of course."

"I brought you some. All the way from Holland. I got it at Hadley's store." Carrie unwrapped the foil from a piece of sweet chocolate and handed the candy to him. He broke it in half, and handed one half back.

"I remember when you used to steal chocolate from Ma's jar, right under her nose," Carrie reminded him. "There's some things I don't forget!" She smiled at him in the dark. "You studied all about it," she said.

"About what?"

"The earth and all. Places like South Hill. And that time you went to the coal fields."

"Well, that's true. It's just *in* me some way. I'm curious to know how long it takes. Millions of years, I guess, with the winds blowing and the land rising and falling and streams filling up and running dry. It's hard to imagine."

"You just get a feeling for it," Carrie said.

"You do," Daniel agreed.

"I remember the time you and me and John ran away," she said.

"And John turned back."

"Because he didn't want to run off too far. That's John, ain't it?" She was silent a moment. Then she added, "I think I always loved you, Danny, since that time, even if I didn't know it. You've always been the most manly boy I know."

"Well! How many boys do you know?"

"I know quite a number," she said quickly. "You're not the only one! I know Little Harry Hadley, who's always sniffing around, as Pa says."

They both laughed.

"You're the only one for me, Carrie."

"You're just trying to get my back into a corner, Daniel Hanson!"

"I mean it. There's something about you that's plainly different."

"My neck is too long!"

"No it ain't. I did a lot of looking at your neck. My eyes fastened on your neck right from the start. It's a real attractive kind of neck, it seems to me. At least it don't look like your pa's."

They both laughed again.

"You look like *your* pa," Carrie said. "Ma always said so. She says you're just like your pa—two peas in a pod. Just as stubborn as a Missouri mule."

"You're right, I guess."

"But you're gentle too."

"Well, I'm gentle, I guess."

"I don't know how one person could be manly and gentle too. But you are that. Just like when Bud caught his leg? Just you and him and John out cutting the south field, so far from the house? And poor John couldn't decide what to do, until you stopped the team and sent John running for Pa?"

"John's okay."

"He always felt second to you, Danny. He told me."

Daniel was silent.

"I don't know why he should feel that," he said. "He's okay."

"Pa couldn't get over it. You just a kid and all, running after that team and then holding Bud's head and being smart enough not to try pulling his leg out of that thresher. Deep down, Pa's got a great respect for you, Danny."

"Bud never forgave me for it."

"Bud didn't?"

Daniel shook his head. "Just wanted to die. Told me he wanted to die, over and over."

"I never knew that!"

"Well, I guess that's between me and him," Daniel said. "Shouldn't have told you."

Carrie fell silent. They could feel each other's presence in the darkness, and see each other's shapes. Only the starlight kept them apart. Outside the old crib the countryside was very still.

"It might be I'll never see you again, Carrie. On account of the war."

"I'll wait. I'll be waiting."

"I could be commended immediately to jail."

"I'll wait," she said firmly. "I can pledge you that."

"Don't pledge anything, Carrie. It's not fair to you—"

"I'll be waiting, Daniel."

After a moment she said, "What do you think will happen?"

"I don't know. They don't have provisions for those opposed to it on the grounds of conscience, or right and wrong."

"They could send you to prison?"

"Or commend me into the Army."

Carrie fell silent again. "Hoovers' won't take eggs from your pa anymore," she said finally. "That's what my pa says."

"Hoovers' won't?"

"That's what Pa says. He says the whole town will get down on you mighty hard for not having the courage to go. He don't see it takes a different kind of courage not to."

"All I know is what I feel," Daniel said. "It's all I got to go on. I can't make any grand arguments for it like we did in school on what's right, the tariff or not."

"How's your pa feel?"

"He's for me, is what he says."

"Is he for the war as well?"

"I guess so. I don't know, when it comes on down to it. He don't talk about it. But he loves this here country, I know that. He always stuck up for the right things."

Carrie was quiet.

"He does harbor a dislike for bosses," Daniel added. "His father was a boss of some kind. There's another thing he don't talk about."

"Maybe your pa's for peace and ain't saying. Saying it just brings trouble."

"I don't know. He'd say, if he had to. He's a scrapper. He's probably for it."

"But he's for *you* too."

"Says he is."

"What about your ma?"

"What about her," Daniel asked.

"She for or against?"

Daniel was silent. "She says I let 'em down. Maybe I did."

"Danny?"

"Yes?"

"You're not letting anybody down, really. I'm proud to know you."

"That sounds like good-bye," Daniel said.

"No, it isn't," she said. "It's not good-bye. That's why I came, Danny. It's not good-bye. I pledge myself to wait. There ought to be one person standing for you."

"There's my pa."

"There ought to be two, then. It ain't easy."

She reached across and touched his face. "I want to give you the strength to do it, Danny. Do you know what I mean?"

"In what way," he asked suddenly.

She pulled him forward. He felt her hair against his face and the softness of her lips against his. He felt the warm shifting burden of her body. He gently kissed her eyes, tasting the salt tears.

And then he held her, to give her strength.

5

Morning was bright and windy. Yellow dust swirled into the air.

Sam Briggs stood at the washstand in his second-floor room over the newspaper office and print shop at one end of Winchester's main street. He looked in the mirror and liked what he saw: a man of middle age with a full head of jet black hair, heavy romantic eyes, and a very noble nose. He was wearing gray trousers and white cotton underwear buttoned down the front. His suspenders hung limply from his waist. He brought the straight razor to his cheek once again and scratched off the last of the shaving soap.

He smiled at the reflection of Miss Mary Cole.

She sat behind him on the edge of the bed. Miss Mary Cole was dressed only in red silk bloomers. She wore bright red lipstick. As she leaned back on the rumpled bedclothes, her long brown hair fell softly around her shoulders. Sam admired her white breasts in the mirror, the soft rounded mound of her stomach, her rose-petal lips.

He glanced back at his own reflection and splashed a palmful of Verona Violette on his cheeks. Then he cleared his throat authoritatively.

"I'm a four-minute man I can talk a mile a minute can you hear me in the back let me hear you if you hear me in the back we've got the *glow* in Old Glory yessir we've got the *free* back in freedom!" he said very quickly, without pausing once.

He took a deep breath.

"I'm ready," Sam Briggs said. "Boy! I'm ready!"

"Well, then, turn around, Sam. Drop your trousers."

The crowd was already beginning to gather on the street below. People had come from the surrounding countryside as well as from the town—old German farmers, tractor salesmen, railroad workers, grain barons, Sunday school teachers, cattle kings, small boys, proud mothers and fathers, well diggers, itinerants, Sunflower Girls. Before long nearly two hundred people milled about in the street. Dozens more filled the two saloons at the south end of town.

Sheriff Bonner and Joseph Webb had installed barricades for traffic. Wagons and automobiles were allowed through one at a time, and were parked every which way along the west side of the street. Flags shimmered in the wind. Simon Turner had put a red cross in the window of his mortuary establishment, in case anyone needed first aid. The reviewing stand, opposite Webb's harness shop and garage, held half a dozen empty chairs. Stretched from window to window above Webb's shop was a long blue and white banner made of silk. It said, WINCHESTER, KANSAS.

William O. Waters peered from his window in the train depot. His old face was lined and furrowed. He watched several boys who had found a ladder and were starting to climb to the roof of the warehouse next to the depot, almost directly across from Webb's garage.

Twenty uniformed soldiers sat at rest among the cottonwoods on the shaded school grounds, just beyond Dr. Homer Pratt's medical office, at the very north edge of town. Behind them, parked in the sun, were the two drab trucks that had brought the soldiers into town from camp. Across the schoolyard the ten members of Winchester's marching band likewise sat in the shade. They wore vivid red and blue uniforms, with brilliant gold braid adorning their hats. Their director, Frisco Fritz, stood among them. He gazed out across the fields, his hands clasped behind his back. He held a short, silver-tipped baton with a tiny American flag attached to it. Only those sitting closest to him could see that his hands were shaking.

Somewhere in town a bell was ringing.

The soldiers got to their feet. Their sergeant, the same who had carried Bull Hadley's regards back to the camp commandant, hummed to himself:

> *'Twas a hell of a war, as I recall,*
> *but a damn sight better than no war at all. . . .*

Suddenly he boomed, "Ten-*SHUN.*"

The tuba played a snatch of "Pack Up Your Troubles." The clarinet played a bit of "When It's All Goin' Out and Nothin' Comin' In," and then switched to "Little Girl, You'll Do." Frisco Fritz put his hand into the air; silence followed, and the marching band took up its position next to the barricades behind the reviewing stand.

Bull Hadley pushed his way through the crowd close to the storefronts.

"Pardon me. Pardon me. Move it, mister. How are you?" he said quickly, even to people he didn't know. He marched up the steps of the reviewing stand, which was now filled with guests, and after a moment spent in pleasantries moved forward to the podium. He grabbed his hat against a sudden gust of wind and looked up the street at a sea of bright faces.

The bell was still ringing. The boys atop the warehouse were waving American flags on long poles. People were pouring into the street from Jack Hurley's saloon and from Mary Lane's, across from Hurley's. They rushed toward the reviewing stand. The crowd seemed to grow larger by the minute.

Bull Hadley waved his silk hat in the air. He turned halfway around and said to the people seated behind him, "This is wonderful! A great day!" Then he turned back to address the crowd.

"Someone you know!" he shouted. "I'll keep it short! Someone you know!" He waved his arms wildly. The crowd quieted.

Hadley leaned toward them. "We're here to have fun," he cried. "We're here for the Liberty Loan!" The crowd cheered. Hadley removed his hat and waved it at the crowd. Then he replaced it on his head. His hands flopped up and down at his sides. "Someone you all know! Certified just last week as a four-minute man! We're mighty proud of him! I'm glad to give you our very own Sam Briggs!"

"Where are you, Sam?" he added.

Sam Briggs arose from his chair on the reviewing stand and moved uncertainly past Bull Hadley. Just as quickly, Hadley descended to the street and began pushing his way toward his store. Briggs gripped the podium with both hands. He stared blindly ahead and cleared his throat. Then he cleared his throat again. There was still no authority in it.

"I'm a four-minute man," Sam Briggs said. "I can talk about a mile a minute. Can you hear me in the back? Hallo?"

The crowd buzzed. Someone hollered, "Louder." Someone else bellowed, "Can't hear him."

"If you hear me in the back, let me know," Sam shouted. His voice cracked, but the crowd roared back. They could hear him. Several hats sprang into the air at the rear of the crowd. Hands reached for the sky. Atop the warehouse American flags waved wildly back and forth.

"We've got the *glow* in Old Glory," Sam cried. "We've got the *freedom* back in freedom!"

The crowd screamed its approval.

After that Sam was all right. He took a deep breath and explained that the triumph of American ideals would mark the death knell of absolutism throughout the world. He told a story about a nurse who was raped by a German soldier in Belgium.

He called for support of the Liberty Loan. He made mention of a young French mother who was forced to watch while a Heinie bayoneted her baby. He said people who refused to fly the flag should be reported to Sheriff Abel Bonner. He said nothing was worth having if it was worth fighting for, and corrected himself. He told a story about three Carmelites in Lisieux who were abused by an entire company of Kraut soldiers. He called upon housewives to use less wheat and more corn, and to go easy on the sugar. He said peace was a great ideal. "That's why we fight," he cried, waving his fist in the air. "That's why you mothers have given this country the greatest Liberty Loan of all—your sons! God bless you! God bless you!" The crowd began to chant. "A fist in the face of the kaiser," Sam yelled. And so on.

This was Sam Briggs's first appearance as a four-minute-man. He did use the words *freedom* and *liberty* at least six times each, while giving his speech the distinctive flavor of his own personality and shaping it to reflect the interests of the region in which he spoke, as suggested by Washington.

"Keep your head down, Fritzie boy," he cried, winding toward a conclusion. "The Yanks are coming! When a Hun yells 'comrade,' stick him with your bayonet!"

He waved to the crowd and pumped his fists up and down in the sultry air. Flags waved back. Fists were raised in the face of the kaiser. The crowd cheered on and on. Sam stepped away from the podium momentarily to swab his brow. At the rear of the crowd an old German farmer gazed at his timepiece and returned it to his pocket. "Seven minutes, forty-seven," he said to no one in particular.

Sam Briggs bounded back to the podium.

"Now for a few lovely songs," he cried. "A musical interlude! Hallo? Now for a few lovely songs, our very own Miss Mary Cole!"

"Someone you know," he added.

Miss Mary Cole, wearing a flowing blue dress and carrying

a single white flower, moved gracefully toward the podium. She clasped her hands before her breasts and began to sing, even before the cheering had stopped.

The hot Kansas sun beat down on her.

The wind gusted and swirled. Her long brown hair went in every direction, winding itself around her face, falling softly to her shoulders, and then rising to wind itself around her face once again. Only her mouth was visible.

The loveliest songs spilled from her rose-petal lips.

"State your name, your current address, and your age," Doc Pratt said.

"My name is Daniel Hanson. I live at South Hill, Winchester, Kansas. I'm twenty-one years of age. I refuse to serve."

"No middle name or initial?"

"No."

"Are you alone this morning?"

"Yes."

"State the place and nation of your birth, if other than the United States of America."

"South Hill."

"You're a citizen?"

"Yes, sir. I am."

"That's obvious. I attended your birth. This is a formality, Daniel, for the record. State the name and current address of the person to be notified in the case of an emergency."

"My mother and father."

"Pete and Livia," Doc Pratt said, turning to Bull Hadley. "Do they know you're here?"

"Yes."

"They chose not to attend?"

"I asked them not to. There's no use of it. It's on my shoulders, not theirs."

"They chose not to attend the parade?" said Bull Hadley.

"My brother is attending," Daniel said.

Hadley closed his eyes like an owl. He sucked deeply on his cigar.

Daniel stood alone in the center of a narrow room on the floor above Hadley's store. Dr. Homer Pratt sat between Bull Hadley and Sheriff Abel Bonner at a long oak table. At the opposite end of the room was an open window overlooking Winchester. The strains of a marching song rose from the street.

Homer Pratt fiddled uncomfortably with a gavel. He had a square, kindly face, and he looked directly at Daniel.

"This is a special hearing, Daniel, called to consider your appearance before this board the other day, when you declared your opposition to serving. I hoped you would reconsider the matter further. Have you?"

"Yes, sir. My conscience don't allow me to feel otherwise."

Bull Hadley removed the cigar from his mouth. "We had boys come in and tell us they belonged to the kingdom of God. Is that what you're saying?"

"No, sir."

"We had boys come in here and tell us they had to stay on the farm on account of weeds and other chores. We had boys tell us of a soreness in the knees that might prevent them from stepping down into a trench. Or that their hearts were faint, and subject to a doctor's care. Is that what you're telling us?"

"No, sir. Not that I know of."

Hadley frowned. "We had boys come in here who were lame and halt, wishing they could go," he said. "And we had a lot of good, loyal patriotic American boys come in here and tell us they were glad to be of service to their country in her time of need. I am obliged to declare that you are far and away the most simpleminded boy ever to appear before this board."

"All I know is what I feel," Daniel said. "I love my country.

I guess I got as much of that patriotic feeling as the next fellow. But war's wrong and so is killing. It's wrong to be a part of it."

"You're making a very hard decision, Daniel, with consequences for all," Doc Pratt said in his kindly voice. "We're a part of all we know and love—"

"You love niggers," Bull Hadley asked abruptly.

Daniel was taken aback. Finally he answered, "Niggers have rights too, I guess."

Hadley smiled. "Not one nigger in the entire state of Kansas has declared himself as opposed to serving his country," he said forcefully. "Eighty-five thousand Kansas niggers, all in the regular Army!"

Doc Pratt's gavel banged loudly on the table. Hadley leaned back in his chair and closed his eyes again. He sucked calmly on his cigar.

"You will not be dissuaded?" Doc Pratt said.

Daniel remained silent.

"We are pretty much restricted to making a determination as to whether you are sincere, Daniel," Pratt explained. "I think you are misguided by your conscience. But I declare you sincere, so far as I can see." He glanced at Sheriff Bonner, who nodded slightly. "Since this board operates on the majority for the greater good of all," Doc Pratt continued, "we are going to register you as a sincere objector, with the notation that this is contrary to your desire. When you get to camp, you will be in the charge of a qualified officer of tact and judgment."

"To camp?" Daniel said.

"I'm sorry, Daniel. We are obliged to order your immediate induction into the United States Army."

"But I refuse to serve. I will not serve—"

"By immediate, I mean you will have to report at Camp Merrill at six o'clock A.M. tomorrow morning."

There was a sudden flurry of movement. Sheriff Abel Bonner rose to his feet; he had not spoken a word during the entire proceeding. Bull Hadley walked around the sheriff and opened the door to the landing, disclosing a uniformed soldier who had been standing outside the whole time. Daniel heard the Winchester marching band strike up another rousing tune.

"This here's Daniel Hanson," someone said.

"This here's Sergeant Gibbons of the United States Army."

"Great day for Winchester, Sergeant. We're subscribing mightily to the Liberty Loan."

"Raise your right hand, son," the sergeant said. "Can you manage that? Say the words I say. Just repeat after me—"

Hadley laughed. "He's slow-witted, Sarge. He don't know what it means to raise his hand up."

Daniel stepped backward. He kept his arms at his side and looked at Doc Pratt, who remained at the table with a faint grimace fixed on his kindly face.

". . . that I will bear true allegiance to the United States of America," the sergeant was saying, "and that I will serve them honestly and faithfully against all their enemies or oppressors whatsoever, and observe and obey the orders of the President of the United States, and the orders of the officers appointed over me, according to the rules and articles for the government of the armies of the United States."

"Congratulations," the sergeant added.

Daniel shook his head.

"It's a mighty solemn oath," Bull Hadley said.

The sergeant threw a burly arm around Daniel's shoulder and turned him away from the others. He walked him over to the window. The crowd still filled the street below. Small boys threw handfuls of gravel into the air and watched the wind separate the fine yellow dust. The sunlight came in golden streamers through the ragged latticework of the warehouse across the way. The marching band had reached the empty speaker's platform and was turning about for another run down the street. Sergeant Gibbons's company of soldiers followed in close order without him.

The sergeant was friendly and understanding. "Morning comes mighty early," he whispered in Daniel's ear. "My recommendation to you, son, is make good use of your time. Pack your bags, kiss your mother good-bye, and find yourself a nice tight piece of ass. May I recommend Miss Mary Cole? She works evenings at Lane's saloon. She's clean as a whistle and knows every trick in the book. She'll even let you jam it up her bunghole if you like." He chuckled softly. "Starting tomorrow, you're at war. If you ain't at camp, you're in prison."

He squeezed Daniel's shoulder in a comradely way.

Half an hour later Daniel walked up the dirt lane at South Hill. His step was slow. His head was down. Livia Hanson sat on the porch watching him through the screen. She kept her hands folded calmly in her lap, not knowing what to expect. Peter stood behind her in the parlor doorway.

"He looks okay," Peter said.

"He's walking slow. He's got a burden."

"He looks okay to me."

"Something's wrong, Peter. I can see it."

"No. He looks okay...."

Daniel crossed the lawn and ascended the porch steps. He pulled open the door. His face was without expression.

"I'm a soldier," he said hoarsely.

The door banged shut behind him.

Livia gasped. "Oh! Thank God!"

6

The plain brown road led over a lip in the prairie and then descended into a swale that seemed to extend for miles. Peter Hanson's wagon rattled to a stop atop the low ridge. Camp Merrill lay spread out in the slanting morning light—the old stone barracks from Indian days, a few weathered gray buildings, a miserable stand of box elder, the sand-and-grass parade ground. To the south were long lines of cavalry stables that had been converted into quarters for recruits. To the north and west lay a metropolis of bleached white tents adrift on the bleached prairie grass.

A faint mist clung to the prairie in the distance. Here and there in the tent city spires of blue-gray smoke rose into the morning air.

"This here will do," Daniel said. "I'll walk on in the remainder of the way."

He stepped down from the wagon and reached for his canvas bag. Peter removed his hat. The two had barely spoken during the long ride from South Hill.

"I don't suppose this causes you to reconsider?"

"I don't suppose *you* ever backed down," Daniel answered.

"No, I never did."

"Well, then, like father and like son." He threw the bag over his shoulder.

"We'll hear from you?"

Daniel nodded. "You can count on it."

"I see," Peter said. He folded his hat in his hands. "You could take the medical service, like the Hofer boys. Or a farm furlough, since it was offered. If things go hard."

Daniel looked at him for a long time.

"I'll be okay," he finally answered. "You'll get along?"

Peter crushed his hat even more tightly. "I'll work that little brother of yours until he gets some meat on him. Then I'll work him twice as hard. Can always hire help if needed."

He put the hat on the seat next to him. It slowly unfolded, like a flower.

"Well, son, you are the best of sons. Good luck."

Daniel reached up and shook his father's hand. Then he shifted the bag on his shoulder and started down the road toward camp. When he looked back, the road was empty. The sun was just breaking over the brow of the prairie.

A short time later Daniel stood at attention in the commandant's office. His shirt was already soaked through. A young lieutenant stood next to the door, arms folded grimly across his chest, feet spread wide apart. The commandant's head was cocked slightly to one side. He stood behind his desk, thumbing through Daniel's papers.

"You refuse to serve," he observed dryly. "You've refused medical service. You've refused quartermaster. You've refused engineers. You've even refused farm furlough. You're aware that Washington has—we encourage boys such as you into the farm furlough program? Consider it. It serves the country, it gets you out of our hair; you don't run the risk of getting shot at." He smiled.

"That wouldn't be fair, sir. That would be slacking."

"You're not slacking?"

"No, sir. I don't believe so. I'm standing up for what I feel is right, is all."

The commandant raised his palm. "No speeches." He rolled his eyes. "Why do all the martyrs refuse to fight? The Army could use a few good martyrs."

He dropped Daniel's papers on his desk.

"I'm obliged to place you in the charge of a qualified officer of tact and judgment. Let me tell you something, Hanson. I have thousands of boys here, willing to be led. I have many officers qualified to lead them. Some of my officers have very good judgment. One or two have tact. But I'm afraid I have no officers with both tact and judgment. I'm sure this is a temporary oversight on Washington's part. In the meanwhile, I'm expected to produce a fighting force. I'm expected to turn bakers and farm boys and bookbinders and tailors into soldiers. There are no regulations to cover absolutists such as yourself, except for this insane order from the secretary. Believe me, if I *had* an officer of tact and judgment he'd be on his way to France to get this war over with."

The commandant leaned forward.

"You'll be restricted to a segregated mess, Hanson. I have three tents of boys like you—socialists, anarchists, Bible bangers. Yellow backs. When Washington decides what to do with you, I'll be the first to tell you. Count on it. I see you've already been given your uniform and kit. It's your responsibility to care for them. You'll be expected to follow orders, even when they don't suit your taste. Is that understood? You'll be expected to salute the flag of the United States of America, no matter how distasteful you find it."

"I don't find it distasteful."

"Do you speak German?" the commandant said.

"No, sir."

"You'll be expected to answer when spoken to. In English. Is that understood?"

"Yes, sir."

"You'll be expected to work. Can you skin potatoes?"

"Yes, sir."

"We'll try to find a potato for you. You'll be given an opportunity to drill. You'll be given an opportunity to join in the defense of your country, should you have a change in heart."

The commandant paused. "I'm obliged to add one thing," he said. "This here is not Winchester. This is not the home place, Hanson, where you write your own rules. This is a military camp. Any attempt to spread your views on the war will be met with swift and summary punishment. Likewise any attempt on your part to undermine the will and morale of the young men in this camp through word or bad example, or any willful disobedience of the legitimate order of any officer. If you're smart, you'll stay out of the way. You'll stick to your own kind and do as you're told. Now, carry on."

"Get your bag. Follow me," the lieutenant added.

"Hanson," the commandant said when Daniel reached the door, "if it was strictly up to me—without Washington, without the politicians, without the War Department, without the niceties of the Military Code—"

"Yes, sir?"

"I'd have you shot."

"But then, I have no tact," the commandant said as the screen door banged shut.

Joseph Webb, who ran the harness shop and garage, sat at the center of the long bar in Hurley's saloon nursing his morning bourbon. He had the place to himself. The tables were pushed into one corner. Chairs were turned upside down on top of them. The freshly scrubbed hardwood floor glistened. Before heading out back with his bucket and mop, Jack Hurley warned Webb good-naturedly to stay on his stool.

Webb barely heard him. He hunched over the bar, carefully

paring his fingernails with a pocketknife. Chips of yellow paint dusted the top of the bar. Webb brushed them away with his arm and turned to contemplate the blaze of light that was Winchester's main street. When Peter Hanson passed by on his old wagon, the harness maker slipped down from the stool and went to stand in the open doorway.

Across the street banners hung limply from the storefronts. There was no breeze. People who had stopped to watch Peter Hanson pass were starting to go back about their business. Curtains fluttered behind open windows above the stores. In the window over Frank Sacco's barbershop, Webb noticed the round blank face of Little Harry Hadley.

Their eyes met for a moment. Then each man looked away.

Webb watched Hanson's wagon. When it was far down the road on its way to South Hill, he lifted the glass of bourbon toward Peter's back. Sunlight caught the rim of the glass as though it were a brilliant jewel, or a tiny spark capable of igniting a conflagration.

"You sonofabitch," Jack Hurley said behind him. He stood with his hands on his hips, glaring at his floor.

Peter Hanson rode in deep silence. Not even the steady creak of the wagon or the tread of Old Don's shoes on the soft dirt road penetrated his thoughts. Peter had realized his error the moment Daniel turned his back on him and set off down the prairie track toward the camp. What he had wanted most, he told himself, was to stand behind Daniel, to support him. What he had done by suggesting the possibility of medical service or farm furlough was to cut the ground out from both of them. He rebuked himself for miles. He felt split in two, as if intention and deed had separated from each other, the strength of love somehow giving birth to weakness. He felt it; he was sure Daniel felt it.

Peter tried to put this out of mind on the long ride home. His eyes fastened on the low pink clouds along the horizon to the east. He listened for the familiar song of the larks. He watched the swallows dive and reel in the morning air. Many of the fields along the way had already been plowed. In others plows and harrows sat at furrow's end, waiting the working light of another day. With harvest done, the cycle of breaking the soil and planting it to wheat and watching it issue forth was about to begin anew—like a giant wheel that turned at its own rate without regard to men or war.

As he came down through the town of Winchester his eyes were half closed against the light. He was oblivious to the figures that walked along the street, and stopped, and turned to stare after him. Not until he was well south of town did he square his shoulders and raise his face. Across the fields, drifting beyond his own stubbly crop of stunted corn, Peter saw the house atop South Hill. The north side of the house—the side facing town—was covered with yellow paint.

He stood up on the buckboard. He snapped the reins on Old Don's misshapen back. The tired horse broke into a trot.

Livia made a helpless little gesture. "They must have come during the night, even before you left. We never heard them," she said. She wiped her hands uncertainly on her apron. Peter stood with his arms folded across his chest. He stepped back and gazed at the side of the house. From just below the second-floor window down to the stone foundation the white clapboard was splattered with vivid patches of yellow paint.

"Of course I couldn't sleep after you and he left. I went out to the porch, so it wasn't then they came. It was earlier, while we slept, Peter. Jamie saw it first this morning—called to me immediately. He wants to paint it over. . . ."

Rivulets of paint had streamed down the side of the house and mixed with the dry soil along the foundation, seeping into the earth.

"We could put him to work on it, Peter. He's old enough. He can hide it with—"

"Leave it be," Peter said. He looked at her. "Do you understand?"

Livia looked away.

Later, after Peter had watered Old Don and Livia had brewed a fresh pot of coffee, they sat in the kitchen. Livia's hands fluttered from her face to her cup to her apron. "As soon as I saw it, I ran for the road," she said. "I'm ashamed to say. It was as though the house—as though it was on fire. But who do you suppose I discovered down to the road?"

Peter looked at her across the table without speaking.

"Mr. Frisco Fritz," Livia answered. "His automobile was parked in the grass off the town road. He asked after you, Peter."

Peter raised an eyebrow.

"He's such a sad little man," Livia added. "I do believe he's not from Frisco. Nor that his name is Fritz."

"He didn't do it," Peter said suddenly.

Livia looked at him in surprise. "Of course not! I don't believe for a moment that he did! He said he'd come by to tell you of the talk in town—the Hoovers won't take our eggs."

Peter considered the news for a moment. "I'll take 'em to Pearl City. It don't surprise me any, considering the Hoovers."

"That's five miles."

"Five miles in the right direction. Away from Winchester."

"It'll hardly pay to go that far, Peter." Livia reached across the table and touched his hand. "Frisco Fritz took one dozen himself."

"Fritz took a dozen?"

"That's right." Livia smiled. "He said it was just between us. He'd gone on down to Pearl City to get strings for his violin and the thought came to him as he passed our place, he'd take one dozen."

"He never took eggs before."

"No, he didn't."

"Who's he going to throw 'em at?"

"Peter! Don't you see? In all these troubles, there's still a hope—"

Peter pushed himself back from the table, cutting her short. "There's a harvest to attend to. I'll have to hire me a man or do it myself. We've got to look forward, Liv. Not back. The Hoovers can go to hell. So can Frisco Fritz. As for the house, I mean it. Leave it be. It means we stand for Daniel. Leave it be as a sign to them as have a hard time understanding that one man is just as important as the next. I won't bend down to anyone."

He turned abruptly and stared out the window, where his son had stood not long before. "The barn's in disrepair as well," he said. "We've plenty to do, Liv—"

"How was he," she asked softly.

Peter was silent a moment before answering. "Resolute."

"Would that I was. Would that I was, Peter. Would that I was the same."

Livia's fears about facing her friends were unfounded. No one called at the Hanson farm on South Hill during the next several days. On the following Tuesday the yard of the Curtis farm was filled with fine buggies and wagons parked in the embracing shade of the old cottonwood.

There the ladies of the neighborhood sewed bandages. And talked.

The north side of the Hanson house remained untouched.

Daniel peeled potatoes his first afternoon in camp. He peeled potatoes all the next day. He diced turnips the following day, and chopped cabbage. Then he peeled potatoes. Each evening he sank into exhausted sleep. His bed was an uncomfortable canvas cot in a wall tent he shared with four other boys, far from the camp headquarters. The tent had a kind of skirting to it, a canvas wainscot held in place by a framework of pine lumber. Resin oozed like honey from the pine. The sides of the tent were rolled and tied at the top with black tape, admitting the hot prairie breeze. Once the last thing Daniel heard before falling asleep were the words of one of his tentmates: "This here prairie's like a prison, ain't it? You can see off in any direction, free as a bird. But ain't none of us free."

"Just mind the rules," another answered.

His tentmates were Eastman, Underhill, Chapman, and Norris. They never used first names. They blended together in Daniel's mind like black and drowsy flies—struck to their soul by the Kansas heat and light but still alert enough to stay out of harm's way when the camp's junior officers strolled through the rows of tents at odd hours to call roll or catch them at a punishable offense. All four were socialists from the East. They opposed the war on the grounds of the brotherhood of man and the solidarity of the working class. But they took to heart the commandant's instruction not to propagate their views. The threat of punishment hung heavy in the air. They talked among themselves of Buffalo, New York, and Scranton, Pennsylvania, and the belles of Birmingham, Alabama. They passed whispered stories of the severity of military justice—men sentenced to twenty years in prison for failing to give an officer a cigarette, men given life terms for reporting back to camp an hour late from leave. And these were good men. These were soldiers, not slackers.

The other boys in Daniel's tent worked, as Daniel did, but not in the kitchen tents. They worked out on the prairie in the sun, grimacing against the light and keeping their mouths shut. Only occasionally did the urgency of their ideas overcome their caution. When night fell and the camp grew quiet, they might lie carelessly on their cots and sing softly together:

Onward, Christian Soldiers,
  March into the War,
Slay your Christian brothers,
  As you've done before.
Plutocratic masters,
  Bid you face the foe,—
Men who never harmed you,
Men you do not know.

But their tent was so far removed from the tents of other recruits, and the singers sang with such soft caution, that their words went unheard.

Each day began with the morning line. Daniel and the others stood stiffly at attention outside the tent while an officer, usually a certain Lieutenant Patterson, strutted up and down the line like a gamecock. Head tilted to one side as though he were the commandant himself, crop slapping against his khaki breeches, the lieutenant would suddenly stop and say, "All men who wish to serve their country—one step forward!"

No one would move.

"All men who admit to the truth that they are yellow dogs, cowardly curs afraid to fight for their country, unwilling to serve the land that gave them birth, slackers and moral cowards—remain at atten-SHUN!"

No one would move.

"Clean up that tent, you assholes! Get to work!"

Daniel's day was spent in the kitchen tents. He tended boiling kettles, skinned potatoes, carefully ran a razor-sharp knife through cabbage and slabs of meat under the sleepy eye of a sergeant who more likely than not had been to Winchester and back during the night. The light and heat blazed in through the open sides of the cook tents. Sweat poured off Daniel's face and chest. When he looked up from his work, the distant prairie seemed to shimmer. From the artillery range came the faint pum-pum-pum of weapons. The sound worked its way into his muscle and blood; it matched its pace to the beat of his heart and the sharp intake of his breath in the stifling heat. He worked, peaceably, to the sound of howitzers.

The boys in the cook tents rarely talked. But one made a point of following Daniel about. Sneed stood at his side at the kettles. He moved with him over to the dicing boards. He was thin. He never wore a shirt.

One afternoon Sneed's eyes darted up to Daniel's, and he said in a heavy whisper, "The Army can go rot. Eh?"

Daniel looked down at him.

"You're one of them that refuse to fight," Sneed said softly. "Eh?"

Daniel didn't answer.

"I'm of the same conviction," Sneed said, his voice dropping even lower. "On what grounds do you oppose?"

"It's wrong, is all," Daniel answered, with equal discretion. "I'm against making people do what they don't believe in. It's something we have to suffer." He kept his head down. His knife was like a metronome, keeping time to the sound of distant gunfire.

"I'm of the same belief," Sneed whispered. "You're Daniel Hanson?"

Daniel nodded. Then Sneed moved away, hauling sacks of flour off a stake wagon and piling them haphazardly on the ground. Soon his shoulders and chest were covered with fine white flour. The next day he did not report to the cook tent. Perhaps to prison, Daniel thought. He resolved to keep even closer to himself.

Day followed day in this fashion. Shadow followed sunlight. Sleep followed a late and hasty meal. The kitchen always ate last. "Just mind the rules," one of his tentmates said. "I see as far as I can see," said another. "I think I see to Colorado. I see to North Dakota. I see clear to the Pecos River, where I never been. But we're like birds that cannot fly, we are. We're like birds with broken wings."

"They'll mend," someone else said. "Sit tight."

"Don't cause a stir."

One morning Daniel received a letter in a plain envelope. The lieutenant handed it to him in the morning line and ordered him to read it. Daniel looked at it a long time before opening the envelope. Then he read the letter to himself. An insurance company in Chicago was offering him a chance to participate in a special "Patriot's Plan" that would protect his mother and father in the event he was called upon to make the ultimate sacrifice in the defense of his country.

He slowly crumpled the paper in his fist.

"Well! She found another boy," the lieutenant declared. "It's hard times everywhere! But you're lucky at that, Hanson. Underhill here's never even got a letter. And Norris either, not that I know of. Chapman got one once, but no one around to read it to him. You ever get a letter, Eastman?"

"No, sir. Not to speak of," Eastman answered, staring straight ahead.

"Yes and no, Eastman. Just answer yes and no. I don't need a speech from someone too dumb to read or write. You never heard from the home folks?"

"Yes and no, sir."

The lieutenant scowled.

Eastman quickly amended his answer. "No, sir. There ain't no home folks."

The lieutenant smiled. "You boys will wise up sooner or later. All the world loves a soldier, that's for sure. But there ain't no one gives a tinker's damn for the likes of you!" He slapped his riding crop smartly against his breeches and began to strut back and forth. The line stiffened. The lieutenant's head tilted to one side. "Clean up the tent, you slackin' bastards! Then get to work." He turned sharply on his heels and stalked away.

"You asshole," Underhill said, taking Eastman firmly by the arm. "You'll get us all sent to the D.B. with that smart talk."

"I'm willing to sacrifice for my ideals," Eastman said.

"Sacrifice yourself. Don't sacrifice me."

Daniel worked twice as hard as usual. Now and then he gazed out through the open flap of the cook tent and watched the drilling squads and companies of recruits in the distance. They looked like tiny centipedes out there, stamping up little dust storms from the parched earth. Daniel's most fervent hope was that the heat and work of the cook tent would overwhelm him, that he would sink to the earth in a faint, that the bleached tents in orderly rows and the dusty drill grounds and the burning Kansas sun would pass from his eyes.

He was stronger than he knew. He grew stronger.

One night after dark three new recruits were brought to Daniel's tent at the edge of the prairie. "We're crowded as is!" Underhill complained.

"Not enough room," Norris added.

"Keep it quiet in there," an officer said from out in the darkness. "We're getting more of you boys than we know what to do with. Now, make a little room there. Is that you, Hanson? Stay where you're at. Move on over to the other side, Chapman. I got three more soldiers here don't want to fight, looking for someplace to hide. . . ."

Daniel's eyes were open. His arms and shoulders ached from a hard day in the kitchen. He watched three looming shadows fill the tent, one nearly blocking the doorway as he entered. The new recruits felt their way past him and began to settle in.

"Sweet dreams," the officer said pleasantly from outside the tent.

"I have sweet treams! I tell you!" one of the newcomers answered loudly in a strong firm voice.

"Let me tell you lads something," one of Daniel's tentmates said after the officer had left. "Mind the rules. Just mind the goddamn rules. We don't want no trouble here."

"Got enough trouble," added another. "Just look how dark

it is out there tonight! You can see way past the stars, I'm sure of it!"

"I tell you," the new recruit agreed dourly. "May Gott preserve us!"

The tent grew quiet.

Soon there was no sound except for the gentle murmuring of the new recruits—saying their prayers.

Daniel woke up with a start. Milky morning light poured into the tent. One of the new recruits towered over his cot. Despite the oppressive heat, the man was dressed in long underwear fastened at the neck. His blond head scraped the top of the tent.

"I am Jacob Decker," he announced. "Here is Joseph Wurz. Here is Peter Knels." He stuck out his huge, callused hand.

Daniel took it and pulled himself into a sitting position.

He introduced himself and the others, and glanced over at Jacob Decker's two companions. Small, dark-haired boys, they sat on the edge of their cots. They looked bewildered, but each managed a quick and nervous smile.

Decker himself looked like he had never smiled in his life. He was a towering giant four or five years older than Daniel. His broad, simple face matched the muscular bulk of the rest of his body. His uncombed hair was the color of straw. His broad nose, the strong high cheekbones, the firm set of his square jaw added to the air of resoluteness that his eyes established. There was something close to wrath in Jacob Decker's eyes.

"What have we here," he asked, waving a giant hand about the tent.

"We have here the United States Army," said one of Daniel's tentmates, making up his cot.

"Pretty soon we have here the lieutenant," said another.

"Do you know where you are," Daniel asked.

"I tink the Army," Jacob said with disdain. He scrutinized Daniel intently. "You look from on the farm too," he added. "Well, I am anyway glad to meet you." He turned away awkwardly and began to dress.

Not long afterward Underhill peered over the wainscoting of the tent. "Here he comes. Both of them." The inmates scrambled out of the tent and hastily formed a line.

With Lieutenant Patterson was the beefy sergeant from the kitchen tents. The sergeant carried a carbine in one hand, and in the other a shapeless package wrapped in brown kraft paper and tied with cord.

Before the lieutenant could give his first order, Jacob Decker drew himself up to his full height. "First of all, I tink I protest even to be in this camp," he announced. He glared at the lieutenant.

The line stirred uncomfortably, but the lieutenant shook this off. His head was already cocked to one side.

"First of all, farm boy, I brought your uniforms." He smiled at Jacob Decker. The sergeant tossed the package toward Wurz and Knels, but they made no attempt to catch it. It fell at their feet. "You other men, at ease," the lieutenant said. "Let's see if these farmers can figure out how to get their pants on."

"I tink I protest to wear this uniform," Jacob Decker said. His face had not changed expression. "I have told the Army in North Dakota. I have told all the soldiers on the train. I protest to be in the Army. I protest to wear this uniform. You should have heard by now. I tink I protest also to use the guns. Do I talk loud enough for you to hear?" He raised his voice. "I tink the same is for Peter and Joseph, who are the same as me. I tell you this first, sir! Go get your boss! I tell it to him!"

Daniel and the others stared straight ahead. They could feel the storm coming.

The lieutenant spread his feet very slowly. He clasped his hands firmly behind his back and glared up at Jacob Decker. "You are being openly defiant of an officer's order. When this inspection is concluded, you will accompany me back to the commandant's headquarters—"

"I tink I do not care for your commandant."

"And you, and you," the lieutenant said, waving his riding crop at Wurz and Knels. Then he locked his arms behind his back again.

"We will all come to atten-SHUN," he said loudly. "All who wish to come to the service of their country will take one step forward."

Jacob Decker suddenly threw his arms high in the air. The lieutenant flinched as though he was about to be struck, but Decker had no such intention. His head jerked back. His mouth opened wide, and he issued a high mournful cry so eerie and shrill that it made Daniel shiver. Then, slowly, he began to dance in place.

He jiggled from side to side. He lifted his feet off the ground and stamped them down heavily in the dust. His hands writhed delicately above his head. In an instant Joseph Wurz and Peter Knels began to do the same. Their own high-pitched keening was added to Jacob's.

The lieutenant barked for silence.

"Mind the rules! Mind the rules!" Underwood hissed through his teeth.

Daniel remained at attention. In the distance he could see the regular recruits stepping from their tents and staring across the prairie toward them. Decker's voice rose and fell. His song carried far out over the prairie. His feet worked like pistons in a strange machine, declaring their opposition to war. One of his hands grasped that of Peter Knels. They danced hand in hand. Peter reached blindly for the hand of Joseph Wurz. The three of them danced even faster.

The lieutenant's face turned a bright crimson. He cocked his head first to one side, then to the other. He paced back and forth, glaring at Jacob Decker.

He stopped.

"Atten-SHUN!"

He resumed pacing.

Jacob's song grew louder. Daniel saw officers running toward them from between the white tents in the distance, and turned his head just as the lieutenant made a slight motion with his riding crop. The sergeant lunged forward, swinging the rifle butt around and crashing it into Jacob's forehead. Jacob staggered backward a few steps. His arms dropped to his side. He fell gradually, landing on his back in the dirt.

Instinctively, Daniel bolted from the line and knelt down beside him. He began to loosen Jacob's plain collar.

"Atten-SHUN," the lieutenant screamed.

Jacob's face was white and pasty. His eyes were open, but gave no clue that he could see. There was already a raised purple welt on his broad forehead. A thin trickle of blood ran down his hairline to the side of his face.

"Atten-SHUN," the lieutenant screamed.

Daniel's fingers trembled. He ripped open Jacob's collar and put his hand under Jacob's head. It was only then that he heard the deep and frightful silence behind him.

He turned about slowly.

The sergeant had stepped back a few paces. He held the carbine across his chest, at the ready, in case Jacob Decker should rise from the ground. The lieutenant was talking in an agitated manner with two officers who had rushed up to join them. More officers were running toward them across the prairie.

"These men are under arrest," the lieutenant was saying. "Yes, yes, all three. So is Hanson. Hanson's under arrest, too."

"What did I do," Daniel asked.

No one answered.

The singing had stopped.

The court-martial was held that very afternoon in a small whitewashed room off the commandant's office. The presiding judge was General Jefferson Davis Towles of Dallas, Texas, who happened to be in camp on an inspection tour. There was only one window in the room. Through this Daniel could see the parade grounds outside and the brilliant light.

Judge Towles had the face of a man who'd been dead fifty years, white paste and paper hardened to a mask that had started to peel and crack. His eyelids were ribbed with tiny purple blood vessels. He sat behind a narrow table at one side of the room, flanked by two camp officers Daniel had never seen before. Daniel and the other three recruits sat across from them on a low bench.

The commandant himself guarded the door.

Testimony was provided by Lieutenant Patterson, who described the willful disobedience of a lawful command, disrespect to an officer, and incitement to riot. The sergeant corroborated all he said. In Daniel's case there was additional testimony. The commandant opened the door to admit Lieutenant James Francis Sneed.

"Young man?" Judge Towles said in a parched voice, after Sneed had been sworn in.

"Two days ago," Sneed began, staring at the floor, "I was approached by Daniel Hanson in the cook tent. He spoke under his breath so as not to be heard. He declared it as his conviction that the war is being prosecuted for the benefit of the ruling class, sir, and as a means of inhibiting the organization of workers in factories and on farms. He stated, as his conviction, the idea that the working men of all nations should cast off the chains of their masters. He declared, in addition, that great things are going on in Russia. Then he solicited my assistance in educating the recruits of Camp Merrill to what he called the real nature of the war, sir."

"What was your response." Judge Towles asked.

"I was shocked. I declared my belief in the honor of our struggle to extend the cause of freedom throughout the world."

"Dismissed," Judge Towles said. Sneed stepped down, saluted, and left the room without looking up. The judge looked across the room at the commandant. "This officer's testimony is considered trustworthy?"

"Yes, sir."

"He seems very young."

"One of our finest," the commandant answered. "He's in the military police, sir. Men younger than he is are dying in France. I have the highest confidence in his abilities as an officer, his tact and his judgment." He smiled slightly to himself.

Judge Towles declared a brief recess, consulting in low tones with the officers on either side. He nodded continually; his head drooped like a tired horse. When he again faced Daniel and the other defendants, his lower lip hung down loosely, revealing his long yellow teeth.

"In the case of Jacob Decker, Joseph Wurz, and Peter Knels, recruits, rise and face the court." He paused while the three rose to their feet. "This court finds you boys guilty of all as charged. I shall take into account the apparent fact that you object to your service on the grounds of religious belief. Therefore you are each sentenced to twenty years imprisonment in the penitentiary at Leavenworth, the Disciplinary Barracks thereof, this sentence to be served in full at hard labor. You boys won't wear the uniform?"

"I tink not!" Jacob declared.

"Be seated."

"I tell you! I tink the glory goes to Gott to make us strong," Jacob declared, even more loudly.

An officer moved away from the wall and started down the aisle.

"I say be seated!" Judge Towles insisted. "In the case of Daniel Hanson, recruit, you will stand and face the court."

Daniel stood.

He could hear the approach of troops outside the commandant's office. They were headed for the parade grounds, singing smartly as they marched. Their words drifted through the open window like a hot and unexpected breeze off the prairie:

Yellow back! Yellow back!
We'll get you when we get back!

The judge strained to be heard. His voice wavered. "This court finds you guilty of all as charged, just as the others. In addition, you are—"

"I only sought to help Jacob Decker," Daniel interrupted. "I should have the right to declare my side."

"Please, son. In addition, you are charged with propagating views inimicable to the best interests of the republic, for which there is no defense in law or religion—"

"What Sneed declared was a lie!" Daniel said.

"Please be quiet—"

"I tink so," Jacob Decker suddenly said. "I tink he only tries to help a fellow soldier. I tell you! I tink this boy's a good soldier!"

The judge scowled across the room at the commandant. "We *will* have order," he declared. The room fell silent.

"I am not immune to righteousness," Judge Towles said after a moment. "It may be that in the history of things, what is judged wrongly today will be judged differently tomorrow. More than one noble idea has been defeated on the battlefield only to live on in the hearts of men. With these speculations the court has nothing to do. Are you a member of a political party?"

"No," Daniel said.

"Are you a German in ancestry or allegiance?"

"No."

"The laws of this republic embody the will and judgment of the people at large, evidenced by the fact that millions of men most willingly follow them, often at great personal sacrifice. Do you understand what I'm saying?"

Daniel was silent.

"Do you have a family of any sort?"

"Yes."

"My most sincere regrets. But I am under the obligations of law. This court sentences you to the most severe term within its power, imprisonment at Leavenworth, the Disciplinary Barracks thereof, this sentence to be served at hard labor for the remainder of your natural life."

"My *life?*"

The judge's dry mouth slowly closed.

Daniel had been at Camp Merrill little more than one week.

During that time Livia Hanson wrote her son a letter. She said that she missed him and loved him. She said that things were as usual on the home place. She said the flies were bad. She said she had baked two apple pies. She said Old Don had pulled up lame but now seemed fully recovered. She said his father was looking forward to the corn harvest and would surely miss him too. She said that since Daniel had left, she had begun to see that his way was filled with hardship and uncertainty, and that without strong principle it was not worth living.

The letter arrived at Camp Merrill the following morning. By then Daniel was gone.

7

Carrie Curtis stood at the cook stove in the Curtis place, stirring the apples for sauce with a long wooden spoon. The kettle was near to a boil. The kitchen was very hot, and the open window over the stove did little to help. It allowed Carrie to look outside where the cut fields burned in the Kansas sun and the south wind kicked up little dust devils in the lane that led off toward the town road. Carrie wore an apron over her thin cotton dress. The apron was covered with tiny red hearts. The sleeves of her dress were pushed up, blousing high on her arms.

With her free hand she brushed a few stray, sticky curls of hair from her forehead. Her gray eyes were impatient. She glanced back over her shoulder at her mother, who sat at the table going through her recipe file.

"We all have choices to make, dear," Millie Curtis said at last. "Your father's choice is that you no longer see Daniel."

"How can *he* make a choice for *me*," Carrie asked.

"We've gone through that. He's your father."

"But I *love* Daniel!"

"So do I, darling. We all do. But with John off to war right now, fighting for our country, your father feels it's just not right for Daniel not to serve as well."

"He's not Daniel's father!"

"No, he's *your* father. I think we've said enough."

"But how can I even *see* Daniel? How do I even know what's happening to him?"

Millie Curtis put her file down on the kitchen table with a sigh. She sat with her back to her daughter and didn't turn around. This family discussion had been going on all week, whenever Old Man Curtis left the house. It led nowhere.

"Those are your father's wishes, dear," Millie said patiently. "I feel we should honor them."

"*You* feel! It's fine for *you* to feel! Daniel's only doing what *he* feels is right! What about the way *he* feels?"

"Daniel's a young boy. He's hardly lived. And you're a young girl. How can he know what's right and what's wrong, Carrie? I do believe that will be all we'll discuss of it."

"By what right can Father say what Daniel should do? He's not a general of the Army! He's not the kaiser! He's not—"

"He's not saying what Daniel should do, dear."

"Of course he is!"

"No. He's saying what *you* should do. That's because he's *your* father, and he cares about you strongly. And, may I remind you, it's *your* brother in the Army. In France."

"His choice, of course."

"We all have choices to make, dear. Your father's choice is that you will no longer have anything to do with Daniel until John comes safely to home."

"Until John comes *home?* Now you're adding to it!"

"We won't discuss it."

Carrie turned back to the steaming kettle, stirring the apple mush in long oval swirls. "I'll thank you to allow me my own choice," she said under her breath.

"That will be enough."

"Do you make *your* own choice?"

"I most certainly do. That will be quite enough."

"Then it was *you* who chose not to invite Daniel's mother when the ladies came to sew bandages," Carrie said.

The kitchen grew quiet.

"You've always been a friend to Mrs. Hanson. And she's been a *steadfast* friend to you. . . ." Millie was silent. Carrie glanced back over her shoulder. "I think it shows an *exceptional* lack of heart not to include her," she added.

Millie turned around to face her daughter. "You don't understand, dear. It's as simple as that. Perhaps you'll have more of an understanding when you're older."

"Don't worry. I understand. Daniel Hanson has more heart than all of the Curtises put together! Including John Matthew, much as I love him."

"That will be all. That will really be quite enough. I declare! You simply don't know when to cease. We won't discuss it a single word further!"

"And *there* goes Daniel Hanson!" Carrie said, turning once again to the window and shaking her curls. "Saving Bud's life when he was *fool* enough to get his leg caught in that thresher! And all Bud Curtis wanted to do was to die! Just to *die!*"

"Bud? Wanted to die?"

Millie Curtis stared at Carrie's back. She waited for an answer.

"You're not going to answer me? You said Bud wanted to die?"

Carrie was silent.

"Are you going to answer me?"

"We won't discuss it," Carrie said.

Old Man Curtis came up the lane in his automobile a short time later. He carried a hank of new rope and a large paper bag of ten-penny nails. When he stepped into the kitchen, his face was crimson. He pulled out a handkerchief and mopped the sweat from his brow and around his neck.

"Well, Mother, you like to hear all the news first!" he said cheerfully. "Soldiers on their way in from camp with some slackers, to put them on the train for the military prison at Leavenworth. Quite an excitement, I should say! Mr. Bull Hadley's getting up a small committee to make a welcome. And I damn near run down that little Hanson boy on the road south from town! So anxious to get on home and hide himself under the covers, hardly paid attention to my automobile. Frightened to death by the prospect of real soldiers, I should say. He hardly knowed which way to turn!" The old man stuffed the wet handkerchief back into the pocket of his overalls. "By God! Too hot for me."

Carrie banged the long wooden spoon on the edge of the kettle to clean it.

"I believe this is done, Mother."

The four prisoners trudged along the dirt road in single file. They were shimmering black silhouettes against the flowing light of late afternoon. Four officers in full military uniform cantered along with them, two on either side along the grassy edges of the road. A boxy Army touring car brought up the rear. It was filled with more soldiers, some of whose boots poked at odd angles from the vehicle's windows. The entire procession was dwarfed by the immense bowl of bright blue sky and the flat Kansas countryside, which extended to the horizon. Streamers of evening clouds had already begun to appear.

From far out on the prairie this looked like a small caravan bound for Samaria or Samarkand. But things are rarely so romantic as they appear from a distance. The prisoners were bound together by a heavy iron chain attached to iron collars around their necks. They were bareheaded. Their shirts and trousers were dark with sweat. Their well-worn boots and pant legs were coated with fine brown dust.

Jacob Decker led the procession, as the largest and the strongest. Daniel followed three or four feet behind. Through the chain that connected him to Jacob, Daniel felt a surge of energy and anger—dissipated only now and then when Jacob muttered calming incomprehensible words to himself. Daniel felt as though he were drifting on the sea with strangers, as though he were being swept along from one rising swell to another without effort of his own and with no port in sight. He fixed his eyes on Jacob's back. He tried to match Jacob's giant stride. Peter Knels and Joseph Wurz were carried along like empty sacks, their feet barely seeming to touch the ground.

Under such circumstances talk was difficult. But Daniel told Jacob something of Winchester and South Hill. Talk of home touched a chord in Jacob Decker. He spoke of Knels Prairie in Dakota, and of his cousins Peter and Joseph, and of their grandfather, Old Jacob, who had come to Dakota many years before to avoid service in the armies of the tsar. The old man had lived to see his churches burned, and his grandsons carried off by soldiers and forced into strange uniforms and allegiances. "It is not America to him, Daniel, who we all love."

"But what of his strong faith?"

Jacob twisted part way around in his neck collar, trying to look at Daniel. "I tink so!" he said. "But for an old man there are many fears. . . ."

They walked across the prairie for hours, stopping only once for a dipper of tepid water and a brief rest. The soldiers gathered near the automobile and left them alone—for all purposes chained to the open prairie. Daniel then told the others of his conversation with Sneed in the cook tent and its harmless nature. He tried to tell them his own simple reasons for refusing to serve, but his tongue was tied. The prairie was an oppressive confessional. "I don't hold to no creed, except to stand for what's right. All I know is what I feel, is all." Knels and Wurz smiled nervously. Jacob was silent. In time an officer approached them with several oily rags from the Army automobile. He had soaked them in water, and he stuffed them under the iron collars of the prisoners to prevent further chafing.

As they struggled stiffly to their feet, Jacob broke his silence. "So? You have never said those things? To have a conscience is a dangerous thing! So is to believe on the Lord! We are all dangerous men, Daniel! I tink so!" He turned his face toward the sun as they resumed their march. His eyes blazed with the same intensity as the prairie light, and his voice boomed out:

> *What cannot change I'll gladly bear!*
> *And to the Lord allegiance swear!*
> *Hold fast, my soul, to God's command!*
> *And take me to the Promised Land!*

"Amen!" said Peter Knels from behind Daniel.

"Amen, Jacob," said Joseph Wurz.

One of the officers kicked his heels into the sides of his mount and cantered on ahead. He turned in his saddle and peered down at Jacob. "Can you sing 'She's a Blue-Eyed Gal from Kalamazoo and There Ain't Nothing She Don't Do'?"

"I tell you! I know this Kalamazoo!"

The prisoners lapsed into silence. The talk belonged to the officers on horseback. They joked back and forth. They spoke of staying overnight in Kansas City after delivering the prisoners to Leavenworth, and the various delights thereof.

Then they too rode in silence toward the town of Winchester.

The crowd met them at the north end of town, along the road near the schoolyard. They came out from the shadows of the cottonwoods and pushed close to the officers on horseback, who had closed ranks tightly to flank the four prisoners. Fifteen or twenty men and half again as many boys from the farms near town crowded around.

"Yellow dogs," someone shouted.

"There's Dan Hanson!"

"Soldier boy! Hey, Soldier Dan! Soldier boy!"

"What'd they do? Where they going," someone asked, striding quickly alongside one of the horses and looking up at the mounted soldier.

The horn of the automobile started to beep.

"Purveying views opposed to the country and disrespecting an officer," the soldier called down. "Stand back now! Get on back! Also, exciting a riot!"

"Hanging's not good enough for 'em!"

"Exciting a riot, did he say?"

"Yellow dogs! Yellow dogs! Yellow dogs!" The crowd chanted in unison as it pushed along with the procession. The driver raced his engine, and the vehicle backfired. The horses were edgy.

"Easy there! Move on back!"

Even though Daniel kept his head down, he could see Frisco Fritz at the forefront of the mob, stumbling along to keep pace with the horses. Frisco's mustache was freshly waxed. It bobbed up and down as he chanted with the rest of the crowd "Yellow dogs! Yellow dogs!" His hands trembled. Bull Hadley walked next to an officer on horseback, glaring at the prisoners. Joseph Webb strode along briskly with a tire iron in hand, as though he might be attacked by the slackers. James Hoover was also on hand, still in his white apron, calling out to the prisoners now and then in his high-pitched voice. On the other side of the cordon of soldiers Daniel saw Mary Lane, her round, red face knotted in anger, her fist raised. She rarely left her saloon during business hours because of her employees' untrustworthiness.

A tomato came sailing over their heads from the direction of Webb's harness shop and garage. It caught one of the soldiers on the shoulder, and the crowd gasped. "Watch your mounts! Hold steady, boys," the officer called out. Another tomato hit Peter Knels squarely in the chest. Daniel heard him cry in surprise and at last looked up to see Guy Martini on the roof of Webb's garage. There was a large paper sack at the cabinetmaker's feet. He reached into it and lobbed still another tomato in Daniel's direction.

"I tink you keep your chin up from these people you know, Daniel! And not to duck," cried Jacob. Every time Daniel moved in a sudden way, Jacob's head snapped back because of the neck collar.

Daniel could no longer hear the horn and constant backfire of the Army automobile. It had stopped on Winchester's main street. The soldiers were piling out and rushing forward to help the mounted officers hold back the crowd as the prisoners moved toward the station. From across the fields to the south of town came the urgent cry of the approaching train. A moment later it glided past the station and came to a stop with a sudden release of steam. "Slackers," someone shouted from the crowd. "Yellow dogs!" someone answered.

The chant began again: "Yellow *dogs!* Yellow *dogs!* Yellow *dogs!* . . ."

One of the officers glanced down at Daniel. He seemed to smile, but whether it was a sign of assurance or a grimace of distaste, Daniel could not tell. For the first time Daniel heard the voice of Sheriff Abel Bonner above the crowd. "Beer at Hurley's," Bonner cried. "Free drinks at Hurley's! Get on home, Harry! Down to Hurley's! Drop that iron, Webb! Beer at Hurley's!" The crowd ignored him, and pressed closer. An officer bounded up the steps of the last railway car and pounded on the yellow door. It opened to reveal the conductor, his hat askew, his eyes round and white. The officer motioned to the men on the platform, someone took Daniel's arm, and prisoners and soldiers were pushed up the steps together.

Daniel was nearly through the door when he heard Carrie's voice drift over the crowd.

"Daniel," she cried. "Daniel Hanson!" She stood on her tiptoes behind the massive form of Little Harry Hadley, barely able to see the prisoners through the crowd. She had run almost the entire way from the Curtis place into town. Her face was bright red. Her curls were plastered against the side of her face.

Each time she tried to move around Little Harry, he stepped sideways to block her view.

She called Daniel's name again, but no one heard. Daniel was tugged forward into the car, the doors closed, and he was gone from view.

The cries of the crowd began to fade. Inside the car the officers directed the four prisoners up the narrow aisle and into the wicker seats next to the windows, one behind the other. The officers took the aisle seats and stretched out their legs. The train jerked forward. In a moment the grove of cottonwoods in the schoolyard slid past, sunlight spilling from the trembling leaves. Then, just as suddenly, all the windows showed was the flat Kansas prairie north of town and the brown dirt road that followed along the railroad tracks.

"Damn lucky to be alive," said one of the officers with an air of relief. He lit a cigarette.

"Everybody loves a soldier," said another.

"I tink so," Jacob Decker answered glumly.

The prisoners pressed their faces to the grimy windows as the train picked up speed. Daniel's eyes followed the empty road as though it could lead him home. About a mile out of town a township road joined the main road from the east. Fences began to mark off the fields in large rectangles.

Daniel stiffened in his seat.

He could see Old Don off to one side of the road ahead, standing patiently in the sunlight, still hitched to the wagon. The train raced forward and Peter and Livia came into view, standing together near the tracks. They shielded their eyes from the low sun. The steam whistle screamed, the shadow of the train fell across their faces, and they scanned the cars as they sped by.

"Don't see him," Peter said.

"Then it wasn't him."

"Don't see him. Do you?"

"It wasn't him, after all."

Daniel twisted about in his seat to look after them just as Jamie stepped from behind Old Don. The boy carried his toy rifle in one hand. In the other he carried a rock. He stepped forward and hurled the rock with all his might at the passing train as the last car cleared.

Then, once again, the hard western light flooded over them all. In an instant, they were gone.

Daniel lay back in his seat and stared at the window. Here and there snakes were draped belly-up over fence rails, to bring rain. Fields were freshly plowed and ready for planting, flags were still flying in trim towns, empty roads turned away from the railroad tracks and disappeared into the hazy distances between the wheat fields. Eventually the vision of his family began to fade, except for Jamie's face: the soft round cheeks, the glistening eyes, the soft mouth pursed as though waiting for a kiss, and the expression of hurt and betrayal as he hurled his rock at the flying train carrying Daniel off to prison.

The train passed Prairie Flower; it passed Fairwater and Elam, Cornucopia and Silver Creek and Slinger; and then vast expanses of prairie in which there were no towns at all. After a time the officer in charge rose to his feet. He touched the low ceiling of the car with his fingers, then reached into his pocket.

"I suppose you boys would like them neck irons off," he asked.

"I tink so! I tell you! For that we are being grateful!"

"No harm," another of the officers said. He, too, lit a cigarette and stretched.

The car was quiet. Soon the light itself bled away, and the train was commended into darkness—four soldiers serving their country, four slackers serving their conscience.

They crossed Kansas, toward the rising moon.

8

Peter and Livia's world changed by small degrees. The loss of Daniel was more than the loss of a willing hand about the place at South Hill. It meant a subtle change in the way each of them addressed the world. It meant a change in the way the world addressed them.

An officer from Camp Merrill was waiting on the porch steps when they returned to South Hill from the railroad tracks north of town.

It was a beautiful evening. The shadows were magenta. The verbena blossoms seemed to glow in the gathering folds of darkness. The officer's motorcycle was parked off to the side of the porch. The chrome of the powerful machine gleamed with as much beauty as the blossom of the verbena. The grass beneath the officer's feet was littered with the stubs of cigarettes. He seemed a nice enough young man. He carried with him the formal papers of Daniel's court-martial, as a courtesy from the camp commander, and an explanation of the events that led up to it. All this he delivered to the parents in as kindly a manner as his tact and judgment would allow.

"Bad meat draws flies," he said. "These are hard times for all. I'd rather be in France myself, making the kaiser dance. I know there's lots of folks as don't support the war. You'd have to be blind not to see it. I ain't aware of how you folks feel yourselves. But he's your boy, after all. I sure wish I could tell you more than I have. Or tell you better. This here's a hard job, bearing bad news."

"Then it *was* him," Livia said.

"Leavenworth?" Peter repeated.

"Yes, sir. That boy of yours is going to be in the Army a good long time, like it or not."

"I can't believe it of him," Livia said, shaking her head. "Actually struck an officer?"

"Something close to that, from my understanding," the officer said. "I don't have the details. You've got 'em there, the particulars, in that packet of papers. All I know is what I heard about the camp and such."

"He didn't want to fight," Peter said. "He was opposed to it, on the grounds of his conscience. His mother and me, we backed him right up. It ain't right to force a man against his conscience. This here ain't Prussia, it's America."

"You're sure right. This here's America. And conscience is a good thing, I guess. All I can say is, he must have got what was coming to him." The officer looked at his boots.

"How can we get him out," Peter asked.

"You mean out from those disciplinary barracks?"

Peter nodded. The officer shrugged. "I guess you could send a postal card to the President. Don't see no other way. Of course, he might become willing to serve. Many have. Or you could wait until the war is won and the boys are home. This here's a genuine court martial under the rules of military justice, following all the legalities. So, I don't know. I just ride the news around, good and bad. Just don't know what to tell you folks that would give some comfort from it. Sometimes the good is bad and the bad turns out to be good after all. I'm real sorry, that's all. It ain't your fault, I guess. I see you got your flag up, which is a far sight better than some. I heard a flag was burned in Emporia! I seen the sticker on your door showing you gave for the Liberty Loan, and I hear you're doing for the Red Cross. Don't see no button on your shirt, but I'll disallow that. That boy of yours might be better off in than out, considering the mood of the country. From what I hear, that D.B. at Leavenworth is run real smooth. Never heard of trouble there or nothing like that. Gee, there ain't really no accounting for it. No way to tell when a boy's going to turn out different than you expect—"

Jamie suddenly stood up, stepped around the officer, and ran into the house. He slammed the door behind him. Peter called for him to come back, but there was no answer.

"I guess I'll be on my way," the officer said graciously.

And so he left. And so they waited. The more Livia thought about the way things had turned out, the more resolute she became. The more Peter thought about what lay ahead, the more silent he grew. For several days he took the eggs on down to Pearl City in the wagon. Each morning he passed the lane leading into the place of Old Man Curtis, whose boy was in the trenches. He never saw anyone along the road. The ride was long and dusty. Old Don, now and then, favored his bad leg. All in all, this proved not economical. Finally Peter suggested that the hens be killed and dressed for market.

"But they're good layers," Livia said.

"You'd best do it, Liv."

"It'd be a shame, Peter. We've always had them."

"You'd best do it this afternoon, Livia. I'll take 'em into Pearl City in the morning."

That same afternoon Livia hitched up Old Don to the wagon and was on her way down the lane toward the town road when Peter called for her. He climbed down from his ladder and walked over to the wagon. His hands and wrists were covered with white paint, and his shirt was splattered.

"Where you bound to, Livia?"

"Kate Hoover's," Livia said. She looked straight ahead. "It's high time someone asked Kate Hoover about it, right off."

Kate Hoover ran her fingers nervously through her hair when Livia walked into the store. They had always been friendly.

"I don't hold it against you, Liv. Not you nor Pete. Every bushel's got a bad apple. But there's a consideration of business we have to attend to. Jim and me been here a long time, just like you and Pete. You've got that farm, we've got this business—which has been pretty good to us, considering all things. But if we were to keep on taking your eggs, Liv, nobody else would trade with me. It's as simple as that."

"Such as whom, might I ask?"

"Such as Mr. Bull Hadley. Such as Joseph Webb and the missus. Such as Mrs. Mary Lane, who stocks all her provisions from us excepting alcohol. Such as Mrs. Jack Hurley, who has considerable influence over Jack, as you may know."

"What makes you think they might not trade?"

"They all told me, in no uncertain terms. This here's all we got, Jim and me. I suppose I should have told you to your face, I surely know I should have, Liv, but I didn't. I guess I didn't have the heart. And I ain't seen you around, is another thing. I don't hold it against you, Liv—Daniel being a slacker. There's just little I can do. I always liked Daniel, but we've got to go along, Jim and me."

"What if I brought you two dozen layers, dressed?"

Kate Hoover glanced back over her shoulder. The store was empty for the moment, except for her and Livia. Still, she chose her words carefully.

"I just couldn't do it, Liv," she said softly. "James is among the most vocal."

Livia's eyes brightened. She straightened herself. "James is a scarecrow!" she said. "*You* wear the pants, and everyone in town knows it. James at his most vocal goes—peep!"

She turned on her heels. Only when she reached the sidewalk did she stop to reconsider what she had said. And to realize that Kate Hoover was the first town person she had spoken with since Daniel declared his refusal to serve.

Peter painted the house white, the trim green. The north side took two coats.

"All because of Daniel," he muttered one day as he climbed slowly down from the ladder. Livia was weeding the flower bed next to the house.

"What's that," she asked.

"All because of Daniel," Peter said in a slightly louder tone of voice. He looked down at her. "I say, we have Daniel to blame, don't we?" he said loudly. Then he walked away.

He tried to hire help. No one was available. So he and Jamie harvested the corn together. They did the north field first. Every time Peter turned about and came down a row of corn toward the house, in his mind's eye he saw the shameful yellow stain of paint spreading across the side. He had done a perfectly fine job of covering it. The house looked clean and well kept, standing proudly on South Hill against the bright blue sky. But whenever Peter looked in its direction his eyes narrowed. The skin drew tight around his mouth. He felt as though he had something hideously wrong with him, a tumor or a goiter for which there was no cure. He had sharp pains in the center of his back between the shoulder blades, driving straight through to his chest.

Working the harvest with Jamie was different from working it with Daniel, even though comparison was hardly fair because of the difference in their age and temperament. Daniel had been strong and fast. He never quit. Daniel and Peter worked well in tandem, silently and efficiently. Jamie was strong, but only for his age. He complained. He whined. He talked. He needed water. He threw himself on the ground between the rows of corn whenever he felt he could go on no longer, which was roughly every fifteen minutes. He had to be watched carefully to keep him from injuring himself in the picker. When he went for water, he was often gone half an hour or more. One time he promised to return within five minutes. Exasperated, Peter found him an hour later in the south field. He was crawling on his belly between two paltry rows of corn, keeping his head low and pulling his canteen along with him. His face was covered with fine brown dust. His toy rifle poked cautiously between the stalks toward the town road.

Peter stood there a long time, feeling the heat from the burning Kansas sun spread slowly across his chest.

Finally he gave up. He harvested the west field by himself. He brought in the barley field alone. He let the south field go, planning to harvest it later for field corn. He began to spend hours in the garden. He made an exhaustive study of the cabbage, noticing the infinite variety of its leaves, the uncertain sense of order that seemed to come from the myriad forms of whorls and curves.

"There *is* no order to it. Not really," he said to Livia one day.

"There is no order to what, Peter?"

"That good would come from bad, I don't believe. But the reverse I know to be true." He walked off aimlessly toward the barn.

Livia found herself in town one day when Frisco Fritz was conducting the band in a patriotic concert beneath the cottonwoods on the school grounds. Jamie was with her. She stood erect off to the side, holding Jamie's hand. She could feel the faces of the crowd turn toward her, and look away, and turn back. No one spoke to her. She kept her eyes on Frisco Fritz. He directed the band with his little baton, the one with the flag attached. His hands shook.

That night Peter and Livia lay side by side in bed, not touching. The house was dark and quiet. They each stared at the ceiling in the stale bedroom.

"It ain't really on his shoulders," Peter said. "It's all decided for him. He's doing just plain what he wants, irregardless."

"Irregardless of what?"

"Irregardless of others. We brought him up to give a care for others, didn't we? I'm just figuring, Liv, somewhere along the line we did something dead wrong."

"You mean irregardless of us?"

"He don't have to hang on here forever. That ain't what I'm saying."

"There's no other place that means to him what South Hill does, Peter. I've heard him say it. That's why he studied the geology of it. To get to know it better, what kind of history it's had, better than anyone. He loves this place."

"I fully expect that he'll strike out on his own one of these days—"

"He's in military prison, Peter, for what he believes. A principle he's holding to."

"Oh, I don't know. Maybe go on to Colorado. Or up to Dakota where it ain't so hot. I fully expect it. I know some way or other we'd lose him. You raise 'em up to lose 'em. Just to lose him *this* way, to have everything brought down on us—I ain't been to Hurley's once since he's been gone, have I? No. I stayed clear of it. I know if I *do* go, someone's going to have a taste of old Pete Hanson's knuckles. One thing I never done is back down. I'll stand for him right or wrong, for his sake. I'm doing it for *his* sake, not going."

"That seems a small price, Peter, to stay away from Jack Hurley's."

"Jack Hurley's all right. Jack Hurley's a working man."

"I'm sure he is."

"There's nothing small about sneaking up in the night and throwing yellow paint on the wall, is there? There's nothing small about having to go ten miles to trade instead of into your own town. Or having folks you always got on with fine treat you like a hand-me-down, just turn their faces away whenever they see you."

Livia reached out and touched Peter's arm in the darkness.

"What if he was willing to serve," Peter asked.

"You mean, go against his conscience?"

"I don't know about conscience, Liv. Never had the luxury to afford it."

"You know more about conscience than any man who ever was, Peter. I've seen you stand up more than once for what you knew in your heart was good and true. You stood for Daniel at a time—you sure do stand up for this family and always have. You're a hard worker, Peter, and a good provider. I've never seen you back off from anyone."

"Well, you're right," he agreed. "I never did."

Their silence filled the bedroom. They could hear the poor-wills through the window screen.

"It might just be that his conscience will get a little wiser," Peter finally said.

"You're the one who encouraged him, Peter. You're the one who told him to run it and all."

"I encouraged him to think for himself. I encouraged him to stand up for what he feels is right. I didn't encourage him not to serve. I didn't encourage him to go against his country to such a large extent."

"It's the same thing, Peter. You can't pick it for him, where he's going to plant his feet and stand. He's our boy after all, as that soldier said. . . ."

Peter and Livia had many conversations. They resolved nothing.

By the time the days turned gray and the nights grew cold, the corn in the south field still stood brown and brittle. It was unharvested.

9

Michael Carr was an objector with privileges. Except for the compromisers who took hospital duty within the prison, and those who finally performed alternate service in order to secure their release, this made Carr one of a kind.

As a civilian he had been a statistician for an insurance company in Fort Wayne. At the U.S. Military Prison and Disciplinary Barracks, Fort Leavenworth, Kansas, he was given the same job. He reported directly to the commandant. He gathered statistics on prisoners, guards, soldiers, officers, bars of soap, books read, meals eaten, hours spent doing this or doing that—anything that could be counted and tabulated. Statistics, the commandant declared, was the wave of the future. This was the way in which men were going to establish efficient control over other men once the war was ended. Numbers can be managed, he liked to say; men, not always so. The commandant considered himself a man of progressive sentiment.

Michael Carr smiled faintly and agreed.

He could have been a tightrope walker in the circus, as well as a statistician. His unassuming manner and acquiescence to the rules of the Disciplinary Barracks earned him the trust of those in charge. So, too, did his pale, almost glossy skin. Porcelain is the least dangerous complexion. His connection with the commandant gave him the run of the prison. Statistics gave him undeniable pleasure. And then there were the causes and ideas to which he gave his wholehearted but secret allegiance, such as the murder of the President and the overthrow of the entire capitalist system. Carr grew a mustache. He was a revolutionary. And he served a quite extraordinary function for the inmates of the barracks without arousing the slightest suspicion on the part of the commandant.

At the moment he was not officially on duty. He lounged in an open doorway at the very end of the sixth wing, looking out with watery blue eyes on the drill yard. It was early morning. From where he stood Michael Carr could see thirty-two military prisoners, one osteopath, one yard officer, two abandoned caissons, seven trees, and the roofs of four houses off the reservation.

The prisoners toed a straight line, with their backs to the barracks. The sun behind them cast long, irregular shadows on the clay, like those of a picket fence that had been warped by time and weather. The prisoners wore blue prison shirts on which numbers had been stenciled with white paint. All were naked from the waist down. Their trousers were bunched around their ankles.

The gnomish osteopath shuffled along in front of the men, examining their genitals. "Skin it back. Milk it down," he said as he moved from one man to the next. "Okay, let me see it. That's good. Skin it back. Milk it down." The prisoners stared impassively at the sergeant, who stood facing them with his arms folded across his chest and a clipboard gripped tightly in one hand. Once a week they were subjected to an examination for venereal diseases, another of the small indignities that made up life in the barracks. This was directed in particular at the religious objectors, most of whom had never been with a woman.

The doctor had a small, birdlike face that seemed to spring from his soiled white frock.

"That's very good, men," he said when he had concluded. "Now my advice is, avoid base thoughts. Never tell each other stories that would bring a blush to the cheek of your sister or your mother. In that way you can avoid carnal desire and the gratification of lust."

"Thanks, Doc," someone said from near the end of the line. The osteopath waved his hand mechanically in the air and seemed to float away toward another wing of the barracks.

The sergeant stepped forward. He squinted at his clipboard and began calling off names: Guardino, Clark, O'Brien, Anderson, Decker, Hanson, Covelli, Gordon, Taylor, Steinmetz, Pinto, Skinitzki, Burgandy Jones, Meyer, Coues, Hackmann, Schwarz, Turner. He took a deep breath and continued. He didn't wait for each man to answer "aye." If the prisoner wasn't standing in line, there was only one other place he could be—suspended by manacles in the hole, with yellow numbers, not white, stenciled on the back of his shirt and the legs of his trousers.

"This morning we will have exercise," the sergeant announced. "But first, do me a favor. Pull up your pants."

The prisoners bent over as one man and hoisted up their trousers. Michael Carr turned and drifted back into the barracks.

"You boys be sure to wash your hands when we're done," the sergeant advised. "Use plenty of soap." He smiled pleasantly.

The eyes of the prisoners shifted toward the open gap between two buildings on their right. Beyond the gap lay a bright yellow prairie. The prairie itself stretched off to the far wall of the prison, seven or eight hundred yards away.

"Eyes front!" the sergeant said. He paused a moment in anticipation. "Go! Get a move on! Haw!"

The prisoners suddenly broke to their right like a herd of spooked cattle, jostling and elbowing each other for position. They raced for the gap between the buildings and the prairie that lay beyond. Daniel quickly took the lead, a step or two ahead of Joseph Marie Covelli. Both knew that the first two or three prisoners through the gap faced the least risk of injury. Daniel's forehead glistened with sweat. His eyes were fixed on the prison wall in the distance. As he dashed onto the prairie, the air filled with the roar of motorcycles coming to life from behind the buildings. In an instant the cyclists leaped out onto the prairie after the milling line of prisoners.

The prisoners began to string out in lengthening chain according to their swiftness and condition—and, perhaps, their resolution. The motorcycles spun and turned and charged at them, flailing streamers of dust up from the dry earth. The soldiers were clad in brown leather helmets and wide goggles to keep the dust from interfering with their vision. Now and then their booted feet shot out to the side in order to control their spinning machines. First one, then another prisoner stumbled and fell on the rough ground. The motorcyclists bore down on them, roaring over their awkward arms and legs and soaring gracefully into the air. Daniel could hear the rising cries of the fallen prisoners behind him. He heard Covelli's excitable voice through the whine of the engines: "You'll make it, Daniel! Come on!" He tried to run even faster, not entirely trusting Covelli. His arms and legs pumped wildly. His chin was raised. His teeth were clenched tightly together, just like the soldiers on the motorcycles.

The morning air was thick with dust and the angry buzz of the cycles. As he neared the wall, Daniel threw himself headlong onto the prairie, as John Curtis had done in preparing for war. He somersaulted and landed in a heap at the base of the high wall. Covelli did the same right behind him. A moment later a trooper roared down the line of the wall with his engine's throttle fully opened. He kicked at both of them with his pointed boot while miraculously maintaining control over his machine. Daniel buried his face in the salt grass and clover. Only the bravest, most malicious soldiers came that close to the prison wall at such high speed. They rarely tested their luck twice.

After the trooper roared past, Daniel raised his head.

The prairie lay under a rising cloud of yellow dust. Fallen prisoners struggled to their feet and staggered blindly forward, seeking the protective angle of the wall. Motorcycles still crisscrossed the field like bees. They swarmed over the helpless. In the distance, in the gap between the two buildings, the sergeant was waving his arms and blowing furiously on his whistle. The exercise was over.

Daniel breathed heavily, trying to slow the trip-hammer of his heart.

He could smell the hot Kansas earth beneath him. He felt the sweat slowly trickling down the back of his sunburned neck. "Bastards!" Covelli hissed under his breath. Daniel wedged himself even more tightly into the small crevice at the base of the wall. He closed his eyes. Once again he felt welling up the memory of his first night in the barracks—a night when the loudest sound of all was silence.

The four of them—Daniel, Jacob, Peter Knels, and Joseph Wurz—disembarked from the train at Leavenworth station and were marched through the dark streets of the town by a contingent of soldiers from the fort. Moonlight lit their way. Dogs danced along the street beside them, raising a din and trying to nip at their heels. The soldiers kicked them away. Here and there a straggler called out encouragement to the soldiers.

The prison loomed out of the darkness like a pale gray-stone ghost. Searchlights swept the empty sky. Once inside, the prisoners were divested of their clothing and given ill-fitting prison uniforms. A thin young man with watery blue eyes made note of their age, their height, their weight, and several other statistics, including the numbers that were stenciled on their uniforms. Daniel's was 12457. The prisoners were separated. Daniel was led to the third wing of the prison by a cheerful guard who carried his thin blanket and a dented tin dipper for him. "This a mighty big jail, with room for all!" the guard said happily. "Yes, sir! Room for all!"

The cell door slammed shut.

A bare electric light bulb in the corridor outside provided the only illumination.

Daniel stood for a moment, looking into the vacant corridor. Then he turned and sat on the floor at the rear of the cell. There wasn't so much as a cot in the cell—only a white bowl, a ceramic pot, and the blanket and dipper the guard brought. Daniel's back pressed against the rear wall of the cell. Cold seemed to seep through the stone. By leaning slightly to the right or left, he could touch the walls of the cell with his fingers. Daniel put his fingers to his face, tracing the lines of his cheeks, his nose, his lips. Then he buried his face in his hands.

He had never felt so alone in his life.

From a distant part of the wing he heard a guard rasping curses at a recalcitrant prisoner. A chorus of whines and complaint rose up from the other inmates and faded away. Daniel listened for Jacob Decker's voice—a prayer, a hymn—but heard nothing. He felt once again as though he were adrift on the ocean, rising and falling on the cold breast of the sea. First there was a sound from somewhere in the cell block, then silence. Then another sound, then a resurgence of silence. The silence was tangible. It was produced by the prisoners as surely as the cries and catcalls were. Sound and silence were in some kind of relationship—like wind and wheat, ocean and earth—one trying to overwhelm the other.

The silence rose like dark water, growing stronger.

When Daniel finally raised his face from his hands, the electric light in the corridor had been turned off. A faint milky gleam came from the guard station at the end of the hall. Daniel listened to the sharp intake of his own breath.

Then silence.

Now and then he heard the abbreviated clanging of a cell door, the rattling of chains, the laughter of a guard.

Then silence.

From near at hand came a low moan that seemed to issue from the stone and steel.

Then silence.

The silence soon flooded over him. It was unlike anything he had ever heard. Unlike the stars at night, unlike the deepest sleep of the house at South Hill. This silence had substance. It was the silence of many men thinking the same thoughts, the silence of expectancy.

The prisoners of the third wing were not asleep. Far from it. Like Daniel, they sat alone or together in their small cells staring at the darkness. Waiting. Daniel did not know what to expect, but finally something came: the sharp, ringing bell of a telephone.

"Burgandy," a prisoner called out from down at the end of the cell block.

The telephone continued to ring.

"Burgandy Jones!"

"Answer that telephone!" came a second voice, closer to Daniel.

The ringing was so real and incessant, so regular, that it took Daniel several moments to realize that it was not a telephone at all. It was an immaculate imitation. Some men could imitate the call of a lark or a grouse, and lure it from its freedom. Here was a man who could imitate the ringing of a telephone, and escape from confinement.

The ringing stopped abruptly. A deep and resonant voice took its place: "Halloo-o-o, Sweetie! This here's Burgandy! How berry nice of you to call!"

It was a gospel singer's voice, sweet and deep and rich, booming through the empty church of every inmate's thoughts. The voice rose and fell like the silence had, overwhelming all that it met.

"My Lord, I do miss you, Rosabelle! Oh honey! The berry same goes with me! I hope you be waiting there for me tonight! Soon that Mistah Mogan fast to sleep I gonna creep right out of this old place, that's for sure and certain! I kiss that ugly man on his cheek soon as I pass by, so he has them sweet dreams and don't wake up no more! Then you and me, Rosabelle my honey, we go on down to Kansas City and that Blue Bell Hotel you knows so well! Tell me I ain't dreaming, honey! We rent that bif soft bed, I'll say, and you gonna get some good old Burgandy after all! Oh, Lord! Same with me, my honey!"

A shudder of anticipation seemed to ripple through the cell block. Every man was wide awake, leaning forward, straining to hear the lilting voice of Mr. Burgandy Jones.

"Rosabelle, you a berry wicked girl," he cried out happily. "I'm glad to hear! Yes, every day brings us more—slackers and such who don't want war no more! We fetched four more today, my honey. Came crawling in tonight! Three's the praying kind and one's a poor old farm boy who don't know right from wrong!"

Daniel sat bolt upright in his cell. But the gospel singer hurried on, his voice now carrying strongly throughout the wing.

"I do hope those boys be listening! And they stay away from Mistah Nelson, who been drinking that bad whiskey once again. And they don't go near that Mistah Hogan, who's nothing but a berry bad disposition with two bandy legs sticking out from a porkpie bottom! And those boys don't *never* truck with Mistah Harold Simms, who dumb as he is ugly! Oh likewise, Rosabelle! You put that good ol' rabbit on the phone!"

He paused for a moment. There was a stirring in the cells.

"Halloo-o-o, Mistah Rabbit! And how's my little bunny? Glad to hear! And how's that war, Mistah Rabbit? What's that? You just a little bunny don't give a care for war? You should be here! Ain't no finer place than this for folks as don't like war! We get lots of carrots, lots of greens—you'd love it, Mistah Rabbit! And now and then we gets a shower, wash off all our cares! You bet! We listens to that skinny man, that boy with eyes of blue and skin what looks like cream! Oh, sure! I'm obliging! You put him on that phone! I be mighty pleased!"

"Goddamn dog," he shouted out in a gravelly voice, as an

aside. There was laughter in the upper tiers. And then the gospel singer's voice turned to honey.

"Halloo-o-o there Mistah Dog! And how are you? I'm glad to hear! You a mighty fine ol' dog if I do say! You give that girl a kiss for this ol' Burgandy, you listening now? Right between them colored legs of hers! That's right! You hear me right, you wicked dog!"

He gargled out a raucous laugh. He resumed with prayer: "O Lord, I prays for Mistah Dog and Mistah Rabbit, that they keep their little noses clean and don't get sent to France. I pray you lets that Mistah Hogan shoot hisself right through his head, 'cause he sure ain't got no heart! I prays as well for Mistah Harold Simms, that he walks into a well and drowns. I prays for all them boys below, who deserve the berry, berry best! I pray you has them new boys listen up to what I says! I makes another prayer for Mistah Dog, that he don't forget to kiss that girl right between them wicked legs! That's right! And how's that, Rosie girl? That's mighty fine! I'm mighty glad to hear! Why, you some girl to wait for this ol' Burgandy. Only ninety-nine more years to go, my honey! I talk to *you* tomorrow!"

The gospel singer's voice was tremulous. When he stopped, there was absolute silence in the cell block. No one stirred. At the end of the corridor a guard by the name of Charles Hogan raised his head sleepily from his desk, turned it slowly to the other side, and put it down on his folded arm. His free hand rested lightly on his holster.

It was long past midnight when Daniel awoke. He had fallen asleep on the floor of the cell with his thin blanket beneath him, dreaming not of home but of his life ahead, in a cold stone prison filled with dangerous strangers.

"Fifty-seven," a whispered voice said insistently. "Fifty-seven—"

Daniel's eyes opened. The corridor was empty. The prison was quiet, except for the faint whisper coming from the adjoining cell.

Daniel recalled with a start that the number painted on his prison uniform ended with a five and a seven. He crawled stiffly to the front of the cell and listened.

All he heard was silence, and the tiny inching sounds of restless men turning in their sleep.

"Yes?" Daniel whispered cautiously.

"What's your name?" came the quick response very close at hand.

"Daniel Hanson," he whispered back.

"Daniel is it? 'God is my judge.' I'm glad to meet you, Daniel. Welcome to the lion's den! My name's Taylor. Otis Judson Taylor."

Daniel tried to shake the sleep and weariness from his head. The whispered voice spoke with the slightest trace of an accent, which Daniel couldn't place.

"German?" he asked. "Russian?"

"No," the voice whispered back. "Harvard."

10

"That's what your name means, Daniel. 'God is my judge.' Not man, but God. I'd almost forgotten," Jud Taylor said after the race across the prairie was concluded and the dust had cleared. The prisoners had been sent out into the fields under the watchful eyes of the guards. "And as God is my judge, you must be the fleetest boy in this prison, the way you run for the wall."

"God has nothing to do with it," Joseph Marie Covelli said.

Jud Taylor didn't look up. He bent over a long row of beans and felt the sun burning directly through his shirt. His aquiline fingers plucked at the waxy beans and flipped them into the gunnysack that trailed along the ground behind him.

"I tend to agree with you, Covelli," Jud Taylor said, after due consideration.

On matters of fact, such as the exact date of the Council of Ephesus, Jud Taylor brooked no opposition. On everything else, including matters of belief and opinion, he had tendencies. He was a tall, bony man in his late twenties, already growing bald —a result, he claimed, only half in jest, of excess mental exertion. Before his conviction he had taught classes in comparative religion and philosophy at a small private school near Marblehead, Massachusetts. His subject matter eroded his faith, and he declared himself an atheist; at least he tended toward atheism. He opposed the war on philosophical grounds, seeing the conflict as a forced passage between two eras in mankind's history, one individualistic, the other collective. His refusal to register for the draft, his refusal to report for physical examination as ordered, his refusal to surrender upon induction—each of these acts was individualistic. The four soldiers and two Marblehead constables who came to his house to arrest him, much to the embarrassment of his parents, were emphatically collective. So, too, was the military judge who sentenced him to life in prison, representing —as he pointed out—"the collective voice and conscience of the loyal citizens of the United States of America."

"And since when does God have anything to do with conscience?" Joseph Marie Covelli muttered. Covelli was working on the next row of beans, several feet ahead of Jud Taylor, who tended toward slowness in the bean field.

"I tell you! Gott has to do with everything!" Jacob Decker said sternly. He and Daniel were working side by side on adjoining rows, twenty feet ahead of the others.

Covelli glanced back under his arm at Jud Taylor and smiled. He had succeeded in making the whale spout. Covelli had a dark, squashed face, partly from his years boxing in Philadelphia.

"You're entitled to your opinion," he called out to Jacob. "I'm entitled to mine. This goddamn bean field happens to be located in a free country."

"It is the prison!" Jacob answered.

"This goddamn *prison* happens to be located in a free country!" Covelli said.

Jacob stopped. He stood straight up.

"Do you must say *gottdamn?*"

"I believe Covelli is sorry, Jake."

"Do you ever smile," Covelli asked sarcastically, without bothering to look up. He knew the answer.

"I tink so! Yes! I tink so!"

But Jacob Decker never smiled. Covelli bent over and

resumed picking beans, noticing out of the corner of his eye that Daniel was now three or four feet ahead of him.

"The quiet one, as usual, leads us all," Jud Taylor said.

Daniel remained silent. In a few short weeks he had already tired of the arguments that seemed to refresh the hours of so many of the prisoners, including the ones he liked the best. Covelli was one of them, an immigrant and anarchist who denied the right of anyone to tell him what to do. He was, he told everyone, an internationalist and a free man. His fate was foretold when he proved this by bloodying the nose of the unfortunate baker who happened to chair the registration board in Trenton, New Jersey. His fate was sealed when he decked an Army captain in training camp with a left hook followed by a right cross and a knee in the groin. His sentence was life. Covelli had mellowed since his release from solitary confinement. The guards still watched him carefully, however, though from a safe distance.

"What were you," Jud Taylor asked them all on one occasion. They understood the question immediately.

"All I ever was was a farmer," Jacob Decker said.

Daniel shrugged. "It's a good thing to be. Your own boss. My father's a farmer."

"I was a student all my life," Taylor said. "I learned to read at quite a precocious age. My nose is thin like this because of books. Once I went to Vienna—"

"Keep your goddamn voice down," Covelli advised. "Why did you go to—pssst?"

"To study philosophy," Jud Taylor whispered. "But I discovered—"

"Yes?"

"The beer and girls were a better school."

"That's nothing!" Covelli said quickly. "I fought Irish Bill to a draw at the Quaker Club even though the referee didn't see it that way. The sonofabitch. Irish Mike."

"I thought you mentioned Irish Bill."

"The referee was Irish Mike, a goddamn sonofabitch."

"Do you must say *gottdamn*, Covelli?"

"Watch your language, Jake," Covelli answered. "They'll make marks next to your name in heaven. I used to be a Wob, that's true. Had a red card, of course. But I burned it. Couldn't stand being bossed about by the working stiffs. I worked on the railroad in Mexico. That's where I read Kropotkin. I been to a lot of places you guys never heard of. I used to sell milk in New York City as a boy. I used to do a lot of things. Hell, you don't want to hear—"

"Yes, we do," Daniel said.

"Naw." Covelli stared at the ground. He crossed his arms tightly around his chest to hide the scars from the chains on his wrists in solitary.

These were young men. As dissimilar as their previous lives appeared, confinement in the barracks forged a bond between them. With his schoolmasterly air, Otis Judson Taylor seemed their natural leader. Covelli had a warm heart, for all his bristling manner. Jacob Decker was always dour, passing the hours in silent prayer. He remained steadfast in his refusal to wear a uniform, even though the officers in the yard took a certain pleasure in ordering him to dress as a recruit. "I do not wear your uniform," he would declare, drawing himself up to his full height. "Get your boss! I tell him!" Once, indeed, the commandant himself passed by. "Leave him be," he said. "For now."

The others looked on Daniel with affection, not only for his disposition but because he had reduced all their own arguments to their simplest terms, right and wrong. He believed he stood for right, and they all believed the same.

They shared a tent on the prison grounds outside the sixth wing. At night the sides were rolled up to admit the air. Searchlights swept the grounds, infused the canvas tent with light, then moved on. Lying on his cot at a certain angle, with one arm half over his eyes to block his field of view, Daniel could imagine a world without walls and watchtowers. He could see the stars that glowed alike over Leavenworth and South Hill.

Daniel's world changed all of a sudden, with a completeness that suggested there would be no further change. Confinement took the place of the blazing light and clear distances of western Kansas. An amalgam of accents took the place of the slow, clear language of the wheat farmers and townspeople in the neighborhood of Winchester.

Watchtowers were set at regular intervals along the high stone walls of the prison. They provided a view outward as well as inward, but they were for the watchers, not the watched. Within the walls were several stone buildings: the power plant, the hospital, various workshops, the guardhouse with its long wooden veranda, the executive headquarters where the commandant pored over Michael Carr's endless tabulations seeking a clue to the nature of the slackers and seditionists committed to his care. He found none. Regulation tents pitched between the wings of the barracks were a recent addition.

The Disciplinary Barracks itself dominated the grounds. Eight great wings radiated outward from its center. Four contained cells for the prisoners. These stretched six tiers above ground, two tiers below—one in the basement, one in the subbasement. The deepest cells held men who opposed not only the war and conscription but the discipline and petty indignities of the prison itself. These men were often chained in darkness, suspended from the dank ceilings. They slept fitfully on wet planks thrown onto the floor.

The other four wings were given over to facilities of a different sort—the barbershop, where the prisoners were shaved twice a week; the supply rooms; the shower rooms; the mess hall, into which fifteen hundred prisoners were crammed at one time, eating in shifts and all facing the same direction. Here, too, the commandant occasionally addressed the prisoners, every speech repeated three times in order to accommodate the entire population of the barracks.

Daniel was moved from the third wing to the fifth wing and, eventually, to the tent that he shared with Jud Taylor, Jacob Decker, and Joseph Marie Covelli. Jake had followed the same progression. Taylor had been in every wing, including the seventh, or honor, wing where the cell doors were often left unlocked. Covelli came to daylight from the hole, where he had been sent for refusing an officer's order to drill.

The barracks were filled with tract passers, tailors, street preachers, farmers, students, sailors, house painters, and union organizers. One was a journalist from Missouri, one a Rhodes scholar, one the son of a prominent judge in Birmingham, Michigan, another a boy who had been adopted by a millionaire. Many were religious objectors, confessors of faiths that forbade the bearing of arms or service in war. Others were classified as political objectors, even if peace were their only politics. Still others were deserters who had been apprehended, men who had falsified their claims before the registration board, soldiers who had violated military regulations. Some were mentally troubled; others were criminals. Mr. Burgandy Jones had killed three of his fellow soldiers in the foxholes of France. No matter what the root of a prisoner's opposition, the judgments of the courts and the courts-martial were swift and harsh.

"Have you heard of Amias Shepard," Jud Taylor asked Daniel one day.

"No."

"He's dead, of course. A mystic. His soul was rapt, aglow with the divine. He sang so softly the words never left his lips. I was interested in him, as a type of course. Watched him about the yard. On his first night here he smashed his watch to pieces on the floor of his cell. Henceforth, for him, time stood still."

"How did he die?"

"I tend to think he was claimed by his own beliefs, Daniel. The bruises on his chest and buttocks proved nothing. Death is willed. So is life."

Most of the men did not ascend beyond the anonymity of the numbers stenciled on their blue shirts and brown trousers.

The regularity of the prison routine assured a certain similarity of hours, days, and weeks. The lights went on in the cell blocks at five A.M. First mess was at six. Drill or exercise in the yard followed. The men were then lined up in large groups and sent in gangs of four to the fields beyond the prison walls, to the coal piles near the power plant, or to the laundry. Dinner was at noon, supper at six. The prisoners were returned to their cells immediately after supper. At eight o'clock they were obligated to stand at the doors of their cells with their arms folded, to be counted. At eight forty-five they were counted again. At nine the cell light went out. At ten the single electric bulbs in the corridors were extinguished. Each night silence and sound struggled for supremacy in the cell blocks, until silence eventually prevailed.

The prisoners in tents felt less sense of confinement. But the regulations remained the same. Day followed day with a dreadful regularity, distinguished only by the latest instance of cruelty or harassment from the guards.

Once a week prisoners were allowed to shower, and received a clean set of clothing. It was then that Michael Carr performed his most valuable service for the barracks inmates. Fifty or sixty men at a time crowded into a single small shower room. Water streamed down upon them; soap lathered up across their shoulders and under their arms; clouds of steam nearly obscured them. And there, moving among the naked bodies with his porcelain skin and pale watery eyes, would be Michael Carr, the objector with privileges.

He brought news from the outside. He memorized the contents of letters that had been opened at the commandant's office before being distributed or discarded, whichever suited the whim of the officer in charge. Michael Carr also carried messages from one prisoner to another, and from one wing of the barracks to another. Sometimes he kited letters, carrying them to the commandant's office. There he dropped them unobserved into the executive mailbag so they would leave the prison without interference. He was even known to have carried messages to and from the hole.

One day near the end of Daniel's first week, Michael Carr brushed against him in the crowded shower stall. Instinctively, Daniel pulled back.

"You're Hanson?"

"Yes."

"You've received a letter from Carrie."

Daniel's eyes slowly widened in surprise. Carr's eyes drifted down Daniel's chest and across his hard, flat abdomen. "She loves you," he said dispassionately. Then he was gone, swallowed by the rising clouds of steam. That was Carr's style. He spoke of people on the outside as though he knew them personally. He pared their messages down to the essentials.

The next afternoon a sergeant approached Daniel at the coal piles. The sergeant ordered him down. "And don't get your tail up, yellow dog!" he added, with a friendly smile. "I've got something here that might interest you."

Daniel descended from the pile, his feet sinking up to the ankles in the small chunks of coal. The sergeant put his arm around Daniel's shoulder and walked him across the yard to the line of latrines next to the guardhouse. There he stepped onto the low wooden platform and opened an outhouse door. He turned around and withdrew a delicate pink envelope from his coat.

He drew the envelope slowly across his lips, savoring it. "Hmmmm! Smells mighty sweet!" The sergeant's eyes twinkled as he looked at the envelope. "Miss Carrie Curtis, of the town of Winchester in Kansas. Do I know her?"

"I think not!" Daniel said. He stepped forward to snatch the letter from the sergeant's hand just as the sergeant let it fall down the open hole of the latrine. The sergeant dropped his trousers and sat down. "I'll be damned," he declared in mock surprise. "Miss Carrie Curtis, down a shit hole! Waiting for an answer, I suppose!" The sergeant leaned forward and grunted.

Daniel's face was covered with coal dust and sweat. He turned and began to walk away.

"Oh, Hanson," the sergeant cooed. Daniel stopped. "You're supposed to be working on that coal heap, are you not? I'd hate to report you as a slacker—"

Daniel resumed walking.

He was already a model prisoner. He wrote each week to his family, the maximum allowed. Each time he enclosed a note to Carrie. The first letter to arrive at South Hill was not his first.

"He says he's being treated well, so not to worry," Livia said. "He says he forgot to mention in his last that he saw us on the road near to the railroad tracks and tried to wave, but the sun prevented us from seeing him."

"His *last?*" Peter said.

"He's eating well, although not so well as at home. He wonders if we've seen Carrie about, and sends the enclosed."

"I seen her," Jamie said. "With Little Harry Hadley. They were on their way to town."

"Is that so? Well, should you see her again, you may give her this." Livia put the note in an envelope, sealed it, and handed it to Jamie.

"Can I read it?"

"You may not."

Peter went out to the back pasture to hack at the weeds, Daniel's job. Across the fields to the south Bud Curtis was driving Old Man Curtis's gasoline-powered tractor, a red Waterloo Boy. Yellow dust wafted into the air behind him.

Livia hitched up Old Don and drove into town.

"My goodness!" Doc Pratt said when she stepped into his office and closed the door behind her. "It's fine to see you, Livia!" He removed his glasses and put them on the desk.

"You're on the registration board, are you not?"

Livia's jaw was firm. She stood with one hand on her hip, looking the doctor in the eye.

"I certainly am, Livia. We tried to do what we could. We offered him farm furlough, as you must know, but he wanted none of it. He's a cocky boy, Livia. We tried our best to keep him clear of trouble. I guess by now I should have been out to your place to have a chat. I most surely should have been—"

"His mail's not coming through."

"His mail?"

"That's right. Not all his mail comes through to us from that military prison."

Doc Pratt studied his hands. "It ain't the board's doing, Livia. That comes on from Pearl City. The carrier comes out from there. No, it's surely not the board's doing. I can tell you that."

Livia was at the door when Doc Pratt stopped her.

"How's Peter," he asked.

"Doing very well."

"Ain't seen him."

"He's doing well."

"Sticks to the place, I suppose."

Livia's hand was on the door.

"I *am* sure glad to see you, Livia. And to hear that things are going well."

"I suppose I'm glad to see you, Doc. Ain't everyone in town has the courage to talk to a lady."

Doc Pratt smiled warmly. He squinted toward the window and reached for his glasses.

"Next time you're in, Livia, would it be an imposition to park that wagon around in back?"

Livia went straight on down to Pearl City and talked to the postmaster, whom she found resting in the barbershop. He assured her nothing would interfere with the delivery of the United States mail so long as he was postmaster.

"U.S. Military Prison, you say? The Disciplinary Barracks?"

"That's correct."

He took her name in the event there was anything he could do. Thereafter letters from Daniel arrived even less frequently.

The nights began to grow longer. One morning there was an implication of coolness in the air. The prisoners were given surplus jackets. The coats were official government issue; many of these heavy blue overcoats were torn and frayed. They had last been worn by Union soldiers in the Civil War.

"I'll be damned, I'm a soldier," Covelli said, slipping into his. The sleeves came down to the knuckles on his hand.

Somebody sneezed.

"Gesundheit," a voice called out.

Everyone laughed nervously.

"We're getting more prisoners all the time," a guard told everyone. "You boys are going to have to double up. And soon we're going to have to break those tents. So don't complain. I'm mighty tired of hearing you boys complain. You'll soon find out what crowded is."

That night, after lights out, Daniel and his tentmates lay

sleepless on their beds. He could hear their breathing and the creaking of their cots.

"We've had it easy, all in all," Daniel said.

"You're right," Covelli answered. "A little light exercise in the fields twelve hours a day, without pay. They treat us like dogs. And more of the same tomorrow."

"Being here in the yard, I mean. Rather than inside."

"It's all the same. It's still a prison."

The side flaps of the tent had been dropped to provide privacy, although the entryway was still tied open. Now and then the entire tent seemed to bloom with light as the spotlight touched it from the prison walls above. Darkness returned as the searchlight swept away across the yard.

"I was delivered a message today by Michael Carr," Daniel announced softly.

"She loves you still."

"My parents have written to the commandant, seeking my release."

There was silence in the tent.

"In a pine box is the only way, lad," Covelli said finally.

"Don't get your hopes up, Daniel," Jud Taylor agreed. "I haven't seen a one let go, save those that agree to serve in one way or another."

"I don't know my own hopes anymore," Daniel confessed.

"You're not thinking of serving," Covelli asked suddenly.

"Can't," Daniel said after a time. "Can't back down. But I think now and then of Amias Shepard, and how he went. Did he have a family?"

Jud Taylor didn't answer.

There seemed to be a restlessness in the yard this night, brought on by—what? The overcoats, grown cold with the memory of boys who wore them at Gettysburg and Manassas? The early darkness? The sameness of their days? The evening was beautiful, full of stars. The number of tents pitched in rows between the wings of the Disciplinary Barracks had increased by more than a hundred. There was no more room. Each tent held four or five prisoners talking quietly of loved ones and of home, or of things lost, or of dreams yet to be. Each tent was like a skiff upon the rolling sea, each with its own mariners' tales. In some there were whispers of war. The prison had begun receiving men direct from the desolate and muddy trenches of France. Men who refused to fight.

Searchlights swept expectantly across the crowded yard.

"Ain't none of us knows for sure what he really hopes, Daniel," Covelli said. His throat was tight. "Hope's a fragile thing. Seems to change from day to day."

"There's comfort in numbers," Daniel said. "We're all standing together."

"I don't know. I never felt so alone as here. Nor so crowded in. It's hard for a free-minded man." After a time, Covelli added, "My mother's dead. Died peaceably and all of a sudden, beneath a trolley in the Bronx. For that she came all the way from Calabria. I gave her lots of grief, I'm sure." His voice had regained its strength. "My father? He's a rum. He wouldn't cross the street for the likes of me, on account of I never did listen to a word he said. A goat like him? A drunken bum? Why, if he did dare to cross the street, I'd knock his bloody head right off! So you're a lucky lad, Daniel, from what I know. You got folks that care about you. You get those letters now and then. You never had no cause to be a nomad, did you? Not like me, running from here to there, hardscrabble all the time, never really getting nowhere."

"I'm not a roamer."

"Hell no, you're not. I heard you talk of it enough—South Hill and all. That's sure your place. I hope that some day you get back. Jake's the same, although he keeps it to himself. Don't you, Jake? And never smiles. To have people as care about you, that's a blessing."

Daniel shrugged his shoulders in the darkness.

"Their letter to the commandant pleaded hardship at home, according to Michael Carr."

"There's plenty around, plenty for all," Covelli said.

"That's the thing that gives me pause."

Far across the yard, some of the inmates had started to sing, so softly it was almost indistinguishable. Singing was a violation of the rules.

"I guess I had the silver spoon," Jud Taylor said. "Not that it makes any great difference. We're all here together, are we not? And why? For standing up against the grain. For being the proudest thing a man can be."

"I'd rather be in Newark," Covelli said.

"I tend to think I'm the only one in the yard who's read Thoreau. Or Hegel. Or Spengler," Jud Taylor added.

"I tend to think I'm glad about that," Covelli said.

"It makes no difference what you know or where you're from. What counts is where you stand. My father's a merchant in Brookline, Massachusetts. My mother's descended from the Otises and Shaws. They've never written—not once in eighteen months. I'm just . . . cast out. So you can see, Covelli, it's all the same."

"You write to them, like Daniel writes to his? I never seen you do it."

"I did for a while," Jud Taylor said. "They never answered. Jacob? You never got a letter either. Daniel here's the only one."

Jacob was silent.

When the light swept the tent again, they could see his great shaggy head pitched back on his boots, which he had folded in half for a pillow. His eyes were open. He was staring at the ceiling of the tent.

"Why do we work," Jacob Decker asked.

From across the yard the sound of men singing became louder. Covelli was the first to notice.

"Will you listen to that!"

"They're singing," Jud Taylor said, sitting up.

"It's dead against the rules. Let's sing!" Covelli said.

Daniel's thoughts had fallen far behind the conversation.

"There's a kind of freedom in our care for each other," he said abruptly.

Covelli laughed. "There is no freedom here."

"Maybe it's in us," Daniel said.

"Listen to that! Goddamn! Excuse me, Jake!" Covelli jumped to his feet and pulled up the side of the tent, giving them all a view of the yard. The song was "America the Beautiful." The words were slow and tremulous. More and more men were joining in.

"Gives me the chills!" Covelli said. "A yellow dog like me!"

Daniel swung his legs over the side of the cot and sat up to get a better view. He was still embarrassed by his inability to express himself as Taylor could or Covelli. He looked out into the brightly illumined yard. Every light was on. Every tent was becalmed. Not a single prisoner could be seen, yet the night air was filled with the growing chorus of mournful voices. The searchlights swept feverishly from tent to tent, occasionally shooting upward into the darkness. Whistles blew from the direction of the guardhouse, and officers poured from their quarters in the distance and raced across the yard between the tents, pulling on their shirts as they ran. Some had already reached the walls and were scrambling up to the towers.

"Goddamn! Goddamn!" Covelli said.

The voices of the prisoners rose and fell, echoed off the darkened cell blocks of the barracks, and grew stronger.

"Maybe it's over!" Covelli said.

Daniel began to sing.

Overhead, like sparks from a dying fire, the stars flew westward on the wind.

II

The war was not yet over.

Peter Hanson walked slowly up the lane that led from the town road to South Hill. He carried a .22-caliber repeating rifle in his right hand. Halfway up the rise the roadway was marked with a line he had made in the gravel with his boot. He stopped there and looked up toward the house. The white clapboard seemed to glow in the afternoon light, an emblem of love. The creepers on the porch screen were at last in flower. He thought to himself: For what is this labor? A few fences, a few frail structures that fall to ruin and desolation, children who fly before the wind.

In idleness or work, his mind was elsewhere. Peter met no one. He spoke with no one off his own land. Even his conversations with Livia grew more and more infrequent. She carried on; he seemed lost.

He wiped the sweat from his forehead.

Then he turned around slowly and knelt on one knee in the gravel lane. He steadied his left arm, and brought the rifle up to his eye. He had placed a tin can on top of a fence post fifty yards distant, at the town road. For some reason he thought of his own father: a blurred motion in the air.

Gently, he squeezed the steel trigger. The tin can flew into the bright air and disappeared into the weeds.

Peter pushed himself to his feet and caught his breath. Then he walked down toward the town road. He moved slowly. When he reached the weeds, he kicked about until he found the can. The bullet had passed clean through, once again. He picked it up and replaced it on the post.

He walked up the lane once more. This time he passed the mark he had made in the gravel, going ten paces beyond. There he made another mark. He turned and knelt. He brought the rifle up to his eye. He held it there a long time, without firing.

Behind him he heard Livia's quiet footsteps. He lowered the gun to his knee but did not turn around.

"Good as ever," he said.

"You or that rifle, Peter?"

"I'd say we're both of us pretty true."

Livia's plain dress came nearly to her ankles. Her face was tired, yet stronger than it had ever been. The commandant's letter was still in her apron pocket. He had explained the absolute authority of courts-martial. He called attention to the sacrifices demanded of a nation at war, and quoted Justice Holmes to good effect. He made a very modest allusion to the liberality of his administration of the U.S. Military Prison and Disciplinary Barracks. He closed with his most cordial regards and an expression of his disappointment that he could offer no prospect of Daniel's release.

Peter brought the rifle back up to his eye and held it steady.

"Do you know, Livia, I can't even remember the face of my own father," he said. "None of his features. As though he never existed. It's what you stand for, after all."

"I do believe you stand for steadfastness, Peter. For faith in your son. I haven't seen that gun in years."

"When two are called from the same family, only one must serve."

"The war must go on a good many years, which I pray that it doesn't, before Jamie's of age. And then I pray that he doesn't go," Livia said.

Gently, he squeezed the steel trigger. The tin can flew into the bright air and disappeared into the weeds.

"My goodness, Peter!"

He forced himself to his feet and stared at her. There was a kind of hard darkness in his eyes.

Carrie Curtis came down the carpeted staircase from her bedroom two steps at a clip. She had just reread Daniel's notes for about the thousandth time. Both of them. She kept them hidden beneath a layer of black hairpins in a pink ceramic pin case on her bureau.

Carrie was wearing a light blue sundress, to show off her brown arms to their best advantage. Her hair was drawn back from her face and tied neatly with a ribbon. She was nearly across the kitchen when Millie Curtis stepped into the room from the parlor. Millie held some mending in her hands.

"You're off for your walk?"

"If you don't mind."

"I declare! You demand more exercise than most boys. We'll have to hitch you to a plow!"

Millie smiled. Carrie didn't.

"Supper will be somewhat early," Millie added. "There's another concert tonight, and your father feels the spirit of song moving through him."

Millie Curtis could not escape the consequences of her kind heart. She was hoping to be not merely motherly, but friendly. As usual, Carried treated her efforts with indifference. All girls eventually grow away from their families—some turning outward, others inward. Carrie seemed to be treading a lonely path inward since the departure of Daniel Hanson. She was polite. She was perfunctory. She still made excellent applesauce. But she was in all things visible to Old Man Curtis and his wife supremely indifferent. She had moved off from her mooring and was well out to sea, and quite independent about it.

Carrie turned toward the door without a word.

"Should you see your brother in the south field, where he is supposed to be, kindly suggest to him that he be in by four o'clock," Millie said tersely.

Carrie pushed open the screen door, crossed the porch, let the house door slam behind her, and started down the steps.

"Prospectin' for gold," Old Man Curtis asked from behind her. He sat on the hind legs of his cane chair, rocking back and forth on the porch. His boots were planted firmly on the porch railing. "You look so pretty, you may just find some."

"If you don't mind, I just might."

"And I suppose you do intend to go to the concert tonight with young Hadley," the old man asked.

"If I'm obliged to. I find him intolerable."

The old man smiled. "I thought you would appreciate to have an escort for the concerts, my dear. You are the most unappreciative girl I've yet set eyes upon. Harold told me he had a real sweet time last week. I encouraged him to call on you again. After all, I *am* your father."

"So you constantly remind me. But after all, I am growing to a woman and I would appreciate to make my own mind up on such matters. I don't even speak to him. He's a fool to think he's having a sweet time when I don't speak a word to him."

"Perhaps he appreciates your presence. Or the sweetness of your personality." The old man stretched his legs. His eyes narrowed. "Carrie, my little friend, let me advise you of something. A boy's place is at his father's side, but he will never come back. That boy Daniel will never return, and you'd best cast him out of your heart."

"I'll be the judge of that," Carrie said. She turned and started to walk away.

"Carrie," Old Man Curtis bellowed.

She continued to walk.

He called again, rising to his feet, and she stopped. "So long as you're my daughter, you will acknowledge when I speak to you."

"I'll always be your daughter, like it or not. May I go?"

Old Man Curtis sank back into his chair.

Carrie continued down the curving lane toward the town road. Off in the south field the gasoline tractor stood alone. Bud Curtis was nowhere to be seen. When she reached the road, Carrie slipped off her sandals and turned north. The warm brown dirt felt good between her toes. As she neared the boundary of her father's vast expanse of wheat fields she crossed the road and cut through the grassy ditch to the old corn crib, where she had met Daniel the night before his appearance at the registration board.

By daylight the crib looked poor and commonplace. It looked far better in the sweet darkness of her dreams.

She found Jamie Hanson on the far side of the crib, away from the road. He sat patiently with his back against the weathered boards and chewed on a long stalk of grass. He looked a little startled to see her, even though he was waiting for her.

"I was dreaming."

"About what?"

"War and all. I wish I could serve, like John is." Jamie rose to his feet. He brushed the dirt off the seat of his overalls. "Ain't no letter this week, Carrie."

"Oh! There ain't?" Her heart sank. "Did he write to your folks?"

Jamie shook his head. Carrie saw a young Daniel in his broad Hanson forehead and his brown eyes. She smiled sweetly.

"All I got is two," she said.

"That's all *we* got," Jamie said. "It could be they don't all come through, Ma says, on account of it's a prison."

"Only once did he mention a letter of mine, and that was by hearsay. I wrote him nine or ten."

"He ain't mentioned. Heard from John?"

"Not in the longest time," Carrie answered. "It's like they both went off together, ain't it? Never to be heard from again." She looked across the fields. But then she smiled again. "I *did* get a card from a boy named Tiger."

Jamie shrugged.

"Maybe next week, is my hope," Carrie said. Before Jamie could realize what was happening, she leaned down and kissed him gently on the forehead, closing her eyes as she did so. Jamie closed his eyes as well, but out of quite different sentiments. When he opened them again he stared past her, far up the road toward town. A horse and wagon were turning out onto the town road from South Hill.

"Looks like my pa," he said. "On his way to town. Ain't that funny?"

Carrie shaded her eyes from the sun. "In what way?"

"He ain't been for a long time, Carrie. It's mostly Ma that goes."

Jack Hurley wiped the back of his hand nervously across his mouth. He ran the fingers of his other hand through his black hair and gave Peter Hanson a wary glance.

"I mean it, Pete. You got that look in your eye. I seen it before and I don't like it. We don't need trouble. This here beer is on the establishment, for the auld lang syne. We always been friends. But you'd best drink it down fast, Pete, and be on your way." Hurley stepped closer. His voice dropped to a whisper. "Them boys mean trouble. You seen 'em—"

"I do believe I'll have something to accompany this down," Peter said. Jack Hurley quickly poured a tumbler of whiskey and placed it on the bar in front of Peter. He backed away.

The other patrons in the saloon began to resume their conversations. Peter could feel the blood pulsing in his temples. He heard talk of slackers and soldier boys and hard times being faced by all. He heard his own name mentioned once, but he vowed not to turn around, never to give in. He fixed his attention on a tall tin can Jack Hurley had set out on the counter behind the bar. The can was filled with small American flags made of stiff paper and affixed to sticks of pine.

He lifted his whiskey and drank it in one gulp. As he did so, he stole a glance in the mirror above the counter.

Little Harry Hadley was still wedged into a corner at the rear of the room, playing a game of Red Dog with two other men. Next to them sat two soldiers from Camp Merrill, waiting for Sergeant Gibbons to return. Four men in overalls sat at the next table. Peter didn't recognize them. They were from farms outside of town, or from Pearl City, or were just passing through. James Kent, the photographic worker, was still sitting alone at the other end of the bar. On the roof of his studio building across the street he had set out ten or twelve photographic frames. He was waiting for the sun to develop his latest portraits, a process that generally took four beers.

The table behind Peter was empty, and that was the most important table of all. Bud Curtis and James Webb, the harness-maker, had been sitting there when Peter entered the saloon a short time earlier. They immediately stalked out of the place with a great show of noise and displeasure, kicking their chairs against the table as they departed. James Hoover and Guy Martini, who had been sitting at the bar, followed suit. Martini required some assistance in getting down from his stool. He required even more assistance in getting through the wide doorway to the street.

Peter Hanson made a fist of his right hand. He clenched it as tightly as he could, and stared at it. It was a strong hand, accustomed to hard labor in the mines and in the mills and in the free fields of western Kansas. The knuckles turned white. Then he relaxed.

He stood up abruptly and finished his beer. He left a dollar on the bar. Conversation stopped. As he headed for the door, he saw Jack Hurley begin to walk toward the front of the saloon behind the bar.

Peter stepped across the sidewalk and down into the bright sunlight of the street without looking to either side. He heard Joseph Webb's voice behind him: "Hanson!"

He stopped. He turned around slowly. Webb lounged against the wall on one side of the doorway with Bud Curtis, whose hat was pulled low over his eyes. James Hoover and Guy Martini stood uncertainly on the other side of the doorway. Webb's sleeves were rolled up above his elbows. His forearms were hard, corded muscle. His eyes gleamed like a ferret.

"You slackin' bastards are all the same," Webb said. "Afraid to speak to the real Americans who fight for their flag."

A smile crept along Bud Curtis's face. "I do believe the old man is as yellow as that misbegotten chicken-hearted poor-excuse of a soldier son he's got, hiding off in prison. Look at him, boys. Fear's got a grip on his heart!"

"You look like a dog away from your hole, Hanson," Webb added. "You'd best run off. The house may need paintin'."

Jack Hurley's face appeared in the window of the saloon and disappeared as quickly.

Tiny beads of sweat broke out on Peter's forehead. His shirt stuck to his shoulders. He drew a line in the soft dirt of the street with the toe of his boot, and stepped back a couple of paces. "I don't back down from the likes of you, Joseph Webb," he said flatly. "I never will." He kicked at the line in the street.

Webb looked at Bud Curtis. Then he stepped off the sidewalk into the street, swinging his long arms loosely. When he neared the line he lunged forward, hoping to catch Peter by surprise. James Hoover cried out from the sidewalk and grabbed Guy Martini's arm, holding him back.

The two men in the street grappled and fell to the ground. They rolled over and over in the dust until Peter had the advantage. He planted his foot out to one side and gathered Webb's shirt collar with one hand. Webb squirmed. With the other hand, Peter smashed the harness maker as hard as he could in the face.

Blood spurted from Webb's nose.

Peter released him and scrambled to his feet. He was already breathing hard. He saw the glare of the light on the road, the flags hanging straight down from the buildings across the way, and then suddenly Joseph Webb was up again, circling him with his fists held high. Blood continued to stream from his nose. His eyes were wild.

"At him, Webb! You got him easy!" Bud Curtis called from the sidewalk.

"Hit him!" James Hoover shrieked. His voice was high and trembly.

Jack Hurley appeared in the doorway again. A small crowd had begun to gather across the street. Hurley saw a stray boy standing with his mouth agape, and shouted for him to fetch the sheriff. The lad quickly headed up the street.

Joseph Webb and Peter Hanson circled each other warily in the middle of the street. Now and then Webb spit blood through his sneering lips. Both men held their fist high. Their faces were covered with sweat and brown dirt from the street.

"You're too old for that, Pete!" Hurley called out.

"Too yellow," Bud Curtis said from beside the door.

"Put 'em down!" Hurley said. "You boys break it up!"

Peter felt his heart pound. He remembered Pittsburgh. He remembered the mills. He remembered all the close dark streets of his youth. He hadn't fought for years, but he hadn't forgotten how. He stepped toward Joseph Webb, feinting with his left hand. Webb winced without even being hit. Peter's eyes narrowed. His mouth was open. He breathed quickly. He feinted again and then again. Each time Webb stepped to the side. Then, once again, Peter aimed a left at the harness maker, lunging forward at the same time with his right fist flying. It landed square on Webb's wet chin and sent him sprawling backward in the street.

Webb lay still.

"He's drunk," Guy Martini shouted. "The yellow dog is drunk!" He waved his arms crazily in the air, as though flies were bothering him. "I can handle that sonofabitch!"

Martini stepped off the sidewalk with shaky legs, nearly falling into the street. He caught his balance and moved forward into the sunlight. His skin was rosy, his eyes soft and unfocused. Peter measured the distance and lunged forward with his right fist once again. Guy Martini crumpled to the street without a word.

Peter turned around quickly and drew another line in the dust. Blood covered his knuckles and wrists. He looked up at Bud Curtis, breathing hard. "Cripple or not, it don't make no difference to me! Bring that grace of God down here in the street where it can be seen!" He motioned Bud Curtis forward and then held his hands erect.

Bud pulled his hat down an inch lower over his eyes. He folded his arms very deliberately. Then he leaned back against the wall and smiled.

"Very well," James Hoover declared. He spun around on his heel and started to walk off up the street toward his store, looking back now and again at Peter.

Peter stood alone in the center of Winchester's main street. He pulled out his handkerchief and wiped the blood from his hands. He mopped the sweat and dirt from his face. His eyes never left Bud Curtis. Then he squared his shoulders and started up the street, walking past Old Don and the wagon, which he had parked in front of the burned-out store next to Hurley's.

James Hoover glanced back, and improved the quickness of his step.

A ragamuffin boy dashed down the street just as Jack Hurley finally stepped down from the sidewalk and Sam Briggs crossed over from his print shop. The lad gasped for breath.

"Ain't no sheriff!" he said. "He ain't there!"

"No sheriff needed," Sam Briggs announced. "I seen it all,

from start to sorry finish. Mr. Pete Hanson's just taken hard advantage of two drinkers unable to defend themselves. He spared a cripple and a grocer."

When Peter pushed open the door to Hadley's store, the widow Murphy looked up in surprise.

"Pete Hanson!" she said. She looked at him sharply and frowned. "You're exerted."

He stalked past her without speaking. At the rear of the store he turned and ascended the stairs. At the landing he pulled open the closed door without knocking.

"Pardon us, *sir!*" Bull Hadley said.

The storekeeper sat behind the long table with Doc Pratt and Sheriff Bonner. There was a look of extreme vexation on his face. Four farm boys stood uncomfortably in the center of the room, facing Sergeant Gibbons. Their hands were raised.

"I'll wait my turn," Peter said softly. He crossed over to the window and stood with his hands firmly behind his back, staring down into the street.

". . . and the orders of the officers appointed over me, according to the rules and articles for the government of the armies of the United States," the sergeant repeated quickly. "Congratulations. Now let me give you a little advice. Morning comes mighty early. My recommendation to you boys is . . ."

A dozen people were gathered in the street in front of Jack Hurley's saloon. Sam Briggs was telling his story for the third time: "I seen it happen. You bet I did! I seen the whole thing. I'm a newspaperman. My job is to see it straight. From where I seen it, Pete Hanson challenged 'em. Called 'em yellow dogs. I heard that! Drew a line in the street right here where I'm standing and dared 'em. Ain't no man gonna back down from that. He caught poor Webb when he wasn't looking. Then he tore off after Martini. Had a real bee in his bonnet. His bloomers was in a real bunch! Sure he was drinkin'. Hell, I'm a four-minute man! I keep my eyes open as to what's going on in this town. Bud Curtis here and Jim Hoover, they had the great good sense to let him make a complete fool out of himself. Just like that boy of his. What's that? Of course I seen it happen. You bet!"

"Took advantage, you say?"

"Certainly did! Neither one touched him!"

Peter could see the low piles of coal next to the railroad tracks across the way. Sunlight shot through the windows and empty spaces of the warehouse as though it were on fire. The air was filled with dust. The quiet time, the brief interval of repose after harvest when the sky grew as pure as rare turquoise or jade, was over.

It was a moment before Peter realized the room was silent. He turned around to find the sergeant and four recruits gone. He felt light-headed, and didn't move from the window.

"Ain't seen you for some time, Pete," Doc Pratt said in a kind voice.

"I aim to sign up," Peter said.

"How's that?"

"I came to town for one reason only. I aim to sign up—"

Bull Hadley threw his head back and laughed. His fist slammed against the table and his great jowls trembled. Peter felt the blood rushing to his face.

"You're somewhat overage, Pete," Doc Pratt said gently.

"Can fight as well as any man. Two from the same family called, one goes. I aim to—I aim to bring Daniel home. . . ."

He clenched his fists and tried to relax them, but his fingers trembled. He clenched his fists again. He forced himself to breathe quickly. The room was stifling. Bull Hadley was wiping his eyes with his fingers.

Sheriff Bonner stood up.

"Pete? You all right?"

"Strong as an ox," Peter said softly.

"Worst thing you can do is shoulder his troubles," the sheriff said. "Biggest mistake you can make. I reminded you of that, Pete. This don't bring him back—"

"—good shot," Peter gasped. "Goddamn good shot—"

"You better sit down, Pete," Doc Pratt said. "You don't look well."

Peter breathed quickly. He felt his chest heave. Momentarily, everything went black. But he focused hard on Sheriff Abel Bonner.

"I'm hard as nails. . . . ."

The walls of the room were blazing white. The heat squeezed him.

"How's that?"

"Speak up, Pete!"

Peter stumbled toward the door. There were tears on his cheeks. He pushed the door open and rushed down the stairs. His legs felt heavy. No one in the room had moved.

"I said, Hallo! Mr. Peter Hanson," the widow Murphy called. She stared. "Are you okay, Pete?"

He plunged blindly past her, pulling open the front door to Hadley's store and stepping out onto the sidewalk. He tried to breathe. The air was hot. The high Kansas sky was the color of milk. Broken shadows fell on the street from the warehouse across the way, pointing straight at his heart.

A moment later a crowd had gathered.

"Get Doc Pratt! He's upstairs!"

"Who is it?"

"Pete Hanson. From out to South Hill."

"What happened?"

"Who is it?"

"Somebody died."

"What is it?"

"I didn't see it."

"A man was shot?"

"Who was shot? Was someone shot?"

"A slacker."

"I don't know, madam! I can't see through 'em!"

"He said someone was shot by a soldier."

"A slacker?"

"Oh, my God! Is he dead?"

"Who is it? Can you see? I can't see."

"Oh, my God! Who shot him?"

"They say Pete Hanson. Out to South Hill."

"Pete Hanson? Oh, my God! Pete Hanson shot him?"

"What happened?"

Doc Pratt looked up. His kindly face was pinched and red. His wire spectacles had slipped down to the tip of his nose. "Instantaneously or sooner," he announced quietly. "His heart. He's gone."

"Get on back!" Sheriff Bonner shouted. "Give him air!"

"He's gone."

"Move on back," the sheriff said. "That's it. That's good. He's gone?"

The crowd started to move away.

"We need someone to help carry him," Sheriff Bonner called out.

But only a few people remained. They, too, moved away. Bull Hadley stood solidly in the doorway of his store. The widow Murphy peered around him. Her face was white.

"Goddamn! I'll do it," Sheriff Bonner said.

Doc Pratt pulled Peter to a sitting position. Sheriff Bonner squatted down behind him on his haunches. He slipped his hands beneath Peter's arms and tottered to his feet. Sweating, he staggered down the empty street toward Simon Turner's with Peter Hanson on his back.

Livia knew without being told. She watched Old Don and the wagon turn onto the lane from the town road. She watched the horse come up the gentle rise of

South Hill toward the house at a broken trot. Jack Hurley was at the reins. His black hair streamed back from his head.

She went through numb motions—comforting Jamie, pretending to be comforted by him in return. There was no comfort. There was no feeling. She drew strength from their absence. Standing alone at the kitchen window, looking out on the bright and empty fields, an odd thought came to her: It was she herself who stood for all.

"It's you and I, James Peter," she said, putting her arm around his small shoulders.

"What of Daniel?"

"It's you and I—and Daniel."

That evening she sat by herself in the parlor of Simon Turner's undertaking establishment. Her back was to the plain pine coffin. Electric candles provided the only illumination. The faint strains of patriotic music drifted through the screen door from the concert on the school-yard grounds. Simon Turner's remembrancer lay open on a table near the door. On the first cream-colored page were four notations, each in a different hand:

a Friend
Stranger
Good-bye Peter
for Daniel

There had been no visitors while Livia was in attendance. She didn't ask Simon Turner who had signed the remembrancer, or when they had come. Turner volunteered no information.

His mustache was freshly waxed. He had taken a bath. He stepped through the curtains at the rear of the carpeted parlor and said, "Considering the heat and so forth, very unusual for this late in the season, and the lack of mourners, to be quite frank about it, may I suggest the prudence of conducting the burial service tomorrow rather than on the day following? The arrangements are included, of course. I would be very happy to attend to it, if you'll permit me."

The next day the coffin lay in the bed of the old wagon.

Old Don pulled southward along the town road toward Pearl City. He favored his bad leg. Turner followed close behind at the wheel of his hearse, driving very slowly. This was Livia's arrangement. She sat erect on the wagon seat, holding the reins loosely in her hand. She wore the trim black suit she had purchased three years earlier for her mother's funeral.

Jamie sat stiffly at her side. His round face was brown as a nut. His eyes were calm.

Halfway to Pearl City the wagon turned off the road and followed a sandy track up a slight rise in the prairie to where it caught the wind. The wagon stopped inside the rusted wrought-iron gate of Kansas Rest Cemetery. Livia could see clear to the horizon, where the rising heat from the fields turned the sky the color of mother-of-pearl. Off to one side the preacher sat on the running board of his automobile, arms on his knees, hands folded. The two diggers had been hired by an associate of Simon Turner. They were farm lads, paid by the hour; they had deferments. They rested patiently on their shovels at the top of the rise.

Simon Turner walked briskly past the wagon. Livia stepped down. The preacher rose to his feet and walked toward them.

"Come on down here and lend a hand," Simon Turner called to the two boys. They stabbed their shovels into the earth and came down the rise in long loping strides. Simon Turner fingered his mustache nervously. He touched his nose, recalling the incident in Hurley's saloon. He glanced over at the preacher.

"Can you give us a hand here, Rev?"

"I'm sorry," the preacher said deliberately. "My hands are clean. My back is bad. I'm not as strong as . . ."

They hoisted the heavy coffin on their shoulders and carried it awkwardly up the rise. The two farm boys took the front. Livia and Simon Turner took the rear. Hay and dirt from the wagon bed spilled down upon their clothes.

The preacher walked behind, making a procession.

When they reached the top of the rise they placed the coffin down on a mound of fresh earth. It tilted precariously. Then it balanced and lay still, at a slight angle. Livia stepped back. Her hand groped behind her for Jamie's. Her eyes didn't leave the clean pine planks of the coffin, cut straight and true by Guy Martini in a sober moment months before.

The wind blew gently in the grass.

The service was perfunctory. The preacher stepped forward, taking care where he placed his feet. He peered down his nose at the small book he had taken from the pocket of his suit coat, and which he now held open in his hands. He cleared his throat, so all could receive his words. Then he spoke a short verse that he valued for the simplicity of its expression and the force of its feeling:

> *My prime of youth is but a frost of cares,*
>   *My feast of joy is but a dish of pain,*
> *My crop of corn is but a field of tares,*
>   *And all my goodes is but vain hope of gain.*
> *The day is fled, and yet I saw no sun,*
> *And now I live, and now my life is done!*
> *My spring is past, and yet it hath not sprung,*
>   *The fruit is dead, and yet the leaves are green,*
> *My youth is past, and yet I am but young,*
>   *I saw the world, and yet I was not seen;*
> *My thread is cut, and yet it is not spun,*
> *And now I live, and now my life is done!*

"How old was the deceased," the preacher asked.

"Pardon me?"

"What age was the deceased?"

"Forty-eight years," Livia replied.

"This is a verse for every age, for it shows us the brevity of life and instructs us as to that brief moment which is ours in which to heed the call of our Redeemer," the preacher explained. "You may be interested to learn that it was written by a young Briton in the year of our Lord 1586, on the very eve of his execution for treason." He smiled. He followed with an abridgment of his standard funeral oration and concluded with a prayer spoken in tones so low they soon merged with the prairie wind.

Livia felt light-headed.

When she opened her eyes, she saw that the preacher was walking back down toward his automobile. The service was over.

"They didn't even say his name," she said softly.

"That's quite okay, ma'am," one of the diggers said. "We'll take 'er from here."

Simon Turner extended his hand. Livia turned away.

Behind her, harsh Kansas light flooded high into the sky. The breeze caught the hem of her skirt and made it tremble. Peter was gone.

At the bottom of the rise, looking up at her, stood Miss Mary Cole.

12

The two women gripped each other tightly by the forearms. It passed for an embrace. They looked into each other's eyes.

"There never was such a man as Peter Hanson," Miss Mary Cole said with considerable feeling.

Livia didn't know what to say. She searched Mary's face—the soft brown hair, her lively eyes, her rose-petal lips. They were as different as two women could be. One was young and easy with men, indifferent to convention, careless of her own reputation. The other was older, worn thin by family, plain faced as a horse, harnessed to hard work and renunciation, ordinary in all respects save the resiliency of her spirit.

"I didn't know if I should come. I don't care a hang for what they say, but I'd hate to have it come down on you, who already lost him. My feeling is, there never was such a man in all of Winchester, even in his hardship. I felt a real kinship to it."

"In what manner?"

"I knew his feelings, standing up to it—what other people say and think. You know as well as I." She looked away.

"Did you ever—sing for him?"

Mary's eyes met Livia's. "No," she said, comprehending the question at once. "Rest assured, I did not. I never sang for the mister."

"Well, then, Mary, I'm glad you came."

"I owed it. I owed it to what I think is right. Ain't a man in town would have stood up for his own like he did." Miss Mary Cole looked up the rise at the diggers. "I'm glad I come, after all."

"Are you . . . 'Stranger'," Livia asked.

"No," Mary Cole said quickly. "Just a friend."

As, indeed, she proved to be.

Livia offered her a ride back into town, not seeing any other conveyance about, but Mary accepted only as far as South Hill, saying she would walk the remaining distance for the sake of Livia's propriety. Jamie sat alone in the back of the wagon, watching the town road recede across the prairie. The two women sat in front.

"How did you come?"

"Prevailed upon a soldier boy, on his way to Pearl City."

"Oh."

They rode in silence for a while. Then Mary told Livia of her girlhood and her hopes, and her sad experience in the St. Louis Conservatory of Music—things she had not spoken of with anyone for a long time.

"Of course he whored around," Sam Briggs announced that night in Hurley's saloon. "Had it straight from Simon Turner himself. Miss Mary Cole was the sole mourner."

"Then he wasn't true to anyone, not man nor woman," his companion said.

"No, sir, you are right. Nor to his country, if you take that boy of his as an example."

Jack Hurley stood at the far end of the bar. His black hair had been combed and patted into place. He said nothing.

In the days that followed Livia Hanson stumbled after Old Don and the plow in the fields of South Hill, turning over the prairie earth and preparing it for seed. The air turned bright and cool; but her thin calico work dress clung to her, and her arms and shoulders and legs had an unaccustomed soreness. She cleaned house, sweeping out dust and shavings that seemed to have accumulated for years. She cooked and mended. She repaired the horse's harness when the leather snapped. She raked the gravel lane and the yard before the barn with such vigor that her hands blistered. She set Jamie to work painting the empty hen house.

Now and then she stopped and raised her hand to her brow and peered off across the prairie. The sun was lower. The wheat farmers were planting. Jamie started back at the town school.

On his first day away Livia felt more alone than ever. She gazed at her tired hands and tried to read the mazy confusion of lines that crossed her palms. Her hands were tanned from work. The lines led nowhere. They ended in callus. That afternoon she noticed an automobile parked in the weeds off the town road, and a tall bony woman walking manfully up the lane toward the house.

"I do hope you're Mrs. Hanson."

"I am that."

"I need a word with you about James Peter. I'm Miss Darby, I should have said. Teacher at the town school."

"I'm afraid he's not come home yet, Miss Darby."

"The word I want is with you. I've had my word with him. I've had several complaints from the children about his fighting. On this, the first day!"

"Do you mean James Peter?"

"And I won't have it. I've cautioned him and I feel obliged to caution you. We depend for our learning on a tolerance of others. The friendships we form in early life help shape our general character. I would be very obliged should you put a rein on him and control his behavior—for the good of the whole. He's otherwise a very quiet boy."

"With whom did he fight?"

"I don't know that he did. All I know is, the other children have complained to me about him. I believe it's best that we prevent it."

"What other children?"

Miss Darby's face became stern. "Names are not needed, Mrs. Hanson," she said coldly.

Livia stepped down onto the lawn to watch the teacher leave. Her car backfired twice before she got it started. Livia, meanwhile, walked around to the barn and called for Jamie. He didn't answer. She walked through the south field, where the unharvested corn stood stiff and dry. He wasn't there. She gazed down the empty town road. Only when she stepped back into the house did she realize she had overlooked the obvious. She went upstairs to Jamie's room. He was in bed with the covers pulled up over his head.

Gently she pulled back the covers. His pillow was wet with tears. The side of his face was scraped and bruised. His nose had been bloodied, but the blood had dried.

Livia kissed him.

"Who did this?"

"I didn't see."

"How did this happen, Jamie?"

"Can't say," he said hesitantly. "Jumped from behind while unawares."

"There *must* have been a reason."

Jamie looked away.

"Miss Darby was just here," Livia said. "Said she had complaints of you fighting from the younger children—"

"It wasn't *me* fighting! It was *them*," Jamie burst out. "And it wasn't younger. It was older! They said Danny's a yellow dog —and I'm a yellow pup afraid to fight. . . ."

Livia sighed. Her face softened. She brushed her fingers tenderly across Jamie's bruised cheek.

"And you stood up for Daniel," she concluded. "I'm proud of you, to stick up for your own. Your father would be proud too. You just lie there. We'll have that cleaned up in no time." She started after some cool water and a towel.

Jamie turned his face to the wall. "Got jumped before I had a chance to," he said softly.

At supper he declared he didn't want to return to school. He could learn just as well at home, reading in a book. Livia disagreed. She predicted he would be left alone if he stayed on his best behavior and ignored the taunts of the older children, who were only repeating what they had heard their elders say, and who bore him no ill will of their own. And perhaps he would make new friends, who could see the bravery beneath his quietude. In addition, she said, it was the law that children his age should attend school, and in a civilized country it was important to give respect to the law.

"What did you think of Miss Darby," she asked.

"Didn't like her."

"I thought she was rather nice," Livia said.

She had covered all the bases. Jamie went to school. Several days later Livia asked him how things were working out. He had brought home no new bruises.

"Okay," he shrugged.

His brown eyes told another story.

He looked from one officer to another without speaking. His lips trembled. His wrists strained against the irons.

They lowered a burlap sack over his head.

The angle between the fifth and sixth wings of the Disciplinary Barracks was still heavy with morning shadow. Peter Knels pressed his shoulder blades against the brick wall as hard as he could, seeking some substance, something solid, in a world flying to pieces. Even with the oat sack on his head and his eyes tightly closed, he could still picture the six soldiers standing at attention before him, rifles pointed in the air.

"One slacker less makes this world a better place to be," the sergeant said loudly.

Peter Knels began to pray.

"On your marks!" the sergeant said.

Another officer stepped up next to the sergeant. He held two short wooden planks, one in either hand, each secured by a leather strap across the back.

"Take your aim!" the sergeant said.

The officer with the pine planks spread his arms apart. Peter Knels began to pray aloud. His legs wobbled. The six soldiers with rifles remained at attention. Their weapons remained pointed upward.

"Fire," the sergeant cried.

The other officer brought the planks together with a resounding slap. The sharp report echoed off the building. Several blackbirds fluttered into the air from the roof. Peter Knels spun violently around against the bricks, as though the force of gunfire had ripped open his heart. His head snapped back convulsively. He collapsed slowly against the wall and slid to the ground trembling. There he wept.

The soldiers smiled. Then they began to laugh.

"My feeling is this," Jud Taylor declared one chill morning as the work gangs were being marched out to the prison fields. "We're each of us individuals with a capacity for good and bad in equal measure, with a sense of right and wrong, first as it benefits us, then as it benefits others. This I take as the *sine qua non*. As opposed to it are society, the masses, commonality—call it what you will. In the collective the capacity for good is diminished, and the capacity for evil is greatly enhanced. What happens is this, Daniel. You become a foot or a finger of the collective beast. You lose authority over your head or heart. You do things you would not otherwise do. I tend to think these soldiers and officers are a prime example of the commonality. They do what they're told to do. Right or wrong doesn't enter into it. How else explain the torture of Peter Knels, or any of the others? How else explain the malice of the motorcycle soldiers? How else explain a sentence of life in prison for a good-hearted boy who disregarded himself out of concern for another? The war is Prussianizing the country, Daniel. It's destroying the notion of individual worth, and making us into one great American beast—millions of booted feet, millions of fingers, millions of triggers. I tend to think these boys aren't bad of themselves. They have small enough chance to be kindly as soldiers. I've seen some take a chance. But in the collective? Bah! I'm an individualist myself. It's on our shoulders after all—to do right, to know good from evil, to speak truth to power. We bear the brunt of it—no one else."

"I'm not so sure of that," Daniel said.

"The oatmeal disagreed with me. The coffee was cold. And I'm gradually losing my powers of thought," Jud Taylor said. He slapped Daniel on the back and laughed.

"Nothing gradual about it," Covelli said from behind.

"Do you understand anything I say, Daniel," Jud Taylor asked.

"It ain't only on our shoulders, even if we try to stand for good," Daniel said. "It rolls off onto others."

The authorities had allowed a letter through to Daniel. After one reading he'd learned the opening lines by heart:

> Your father is dead, God rest his soul. He carried us on his shoulders, Daniel. It falls to us to carry on alone. How he loved you! I see you in him and him in you. Both doubters, and yet blessed with kindness and a care for others. He passed quickly and in his full strength near to Hadley's store. Death was due to the heart according to Mr. Turner. We had twenty-four years, more than half my life and precisely one half of his. He's buried in that rise on the west side of the town road as you go on down to Pearl City. There he has wind, sun and the elements as at South Hill. He was attended by, among others, a person who signed the remembrancer in your behalf. I suspect this was C.? but have not myself seen her. Jamie however has carried your notes to her such as we have received. He resumes school very shortly. I am part done with plowing north. O Daniel this hardship,

may I have the strength to go forward. I often repeat your name. I call to mind your father's face which I recollect in exceeding clarity, such was the power of his love for us. At night my poor hand reaches out for him. . . .

The letter was eleven pages long. Both sides of each sheet were filled with Livia's small, firm script.

The commandant sat at his desk wrapped in a greatcoat while the contractor from town worked on the radiators. Michael Carr leaned against the wall and smoked one of the commandant's cigars. Spread out on the desk before the commandant were dozens of slips of paper showing gallons of soup consumed, hours spent in the potato fields, number of boots issued, haircuts given, admissions to the prison hospital, complaints filed by guards and officers against the prisoners.

"You realize that it was not merely an echo," Michael Carr said. "The prisoners in the barracks joined in as soon as they heard the prisoners in the yard singing."

"Actually," the commandant said, "we have three-hundred and ninety-seven objectors on the grounds of conscience. The remainder are criminals, deviates, soldiers who have violated regular discipline, and those with disordered minds."

"I don't believe it can be explained statistically, sir. The song united them, despite their differences. The song was one they all knew. Of course it was an act of rebellion, and violated the rules of silence. But you won't find the answer in numbers. They consider themselves Americans, unjustly imprisoned by their own government—"

The Commandant scratched the nape of his neck. "For murder? For rape?"

"No, sir. The objectors in particular. Some have an excellent education. And whatever else may be said against them, they have been judged sincere by their local boards."

"They are absolutists in an age of change," the commandant said. "They are worse than the Prussians, don't you think? We have fed them well. We have kept them occupied with useful work. We've attended to their various needs. Our administration has been very liberal." He shuffled through the slips of paper on his desk. "Have you kept track of the books removed from the library? They're allowed one a week, aren't they? Perhaps that is too many. Perhaps we are *too* liberal. We don't have to worry about novels and stories. They help pass the time and amuse the men. But facts can be misinterpreted and misunderstood. They can be turned to the wrong use. You might look into this, Carr. Where did the books in our library come from? Which inmates actually borrow books, and which books do they borrow? There may be ringleaders. Men removed from society and placed in prison should have *some* constraints placed on the material they're allowed to read."

"Yes, sir. I'll look into it. An excellent idea."

"Excellent, excellent."

The commandant called his aide into the office. Michael Carr departed. He paused a moment to relight his cigar in the anteroom. There he reached into his coat pocket, withdrew four envelopes, and dropped them into the headquarters mailbag without being seen.

Since that late-summer evening when the prisoners joined in song the commandant had been nagged by bad thoughts. The prisoners under his progressive care might prove to be unmanageable. It was enough to disturb his sleep. He spent hours over his slips of statistics, hoping to find the roots of rebellion before they sent up shoots. The spontaneous singing had thrown a fright into guards and officers alike. It was no longer unusual to see a prisoner being dragged across the yard by his feet or his hair to instill a proper regard for the distinction between keepers and kept. Nor was it unusual for a prisoner to be grabbed randomly by soldiers and suspended head first in one of the huge circular water tanks on the prison grounds, until he was half drowned and entirely docile. Beatings increased. So did the mock executions. Charles Hogan, the guard, was found one evening under the veranda of the guardhouse with a broken jaw. The objectors blamed the murder gang. The murder gang blamed the objectors. Charles Hogan blamed James Nelson, another guard. But as his jaw was broken, he kept his mouth shut.

The weekly motorcycle chases continued. One week, after rain had softened the prairie and created large bogs of mud, the yard sergeant suggested that the exercise be canceled, so no harm would befall the soldiers. "Oh, no," the motorcycle commander said. "The boys need work. Wars are not fought only in sunshine. Glad to help." Another time, most of the objectors were marched under heavy guard outside the prison grounds to witness the hanging of three black soldiers from Kansas City who had raped a white waitress. Several companies of black troops had been assembled at the gallows for the same object lesson. The condemned men wove an eerie cacophony of prayer as they ascended the gallows steps. The traps were sprung, the ropes cracked taut, and the colored troops turned their faces away almost as one man. "We're all niggers," Jud Taylor announced on the way back to the barracks. "Don't forget it."

Jacob Decker grew more and more distant. He never joked. He never smiled or laughed. He rarely spoke. His eyes seemed fixed on some distant scene denied to the others. The pages of his pocket Bible began to wear thin. The soldiers harassed him almost every day. They made him stand at attention in the yard. They ordered him to wear an Army uniform. He refused. But he no longer barked back at the soldiers, "Get your boss. I tell him! I tink so!" He remained silent, glowering at them with a kind of harsh Old Testament judgment in his eyes.

Joseph Marie Covelli, on the other hand, seemed to grow more voluble and cutting. He spoke incessantly of his mother and the sacrifices she had made for him, of his girlfriends, of the time he shipped to sea. He recounted the history of every fight he ever lost. Somehow this put more fire back in his eye.

"I'm best when my back's against the wall," he said.

"Don't worry about it, Covelli."

"Yeah? We need a goddamn revolution, is what I'm saying."

"Against whom?"

"Everyone. Everything."

The boys had to rearrange the inside of their tent to make room for two new prisoners. One was Jack Burton, a young flier with dark, nervous eyes. He loved war. He'd flown twenty-four missions with the Air Force in France. On the twenty-fifth he watched two of his buddies go down in flames, their lives and honor ending in lazy black spirals over the medieval countryside. When he returned safely, he realized that he no longer knew any of the boys he was flying with. The boys he had started with in Texas were dead. He deserted, made his way to England from Calais, and was arrested two weeks later in Liverpool. The court-martial found him guilty enough to pass the remainder of his life in prison, a circumstance he blamed on the fact that the war was being run by pacifists.

"You mean the war is being conducted by men who are opposed to war," Daniel asked.

"Absolutely."

Every day Jack Burton applied to the yard sergeant for reassignment to combat in a pursuit squadron. The sergeant laughed at him.

"I've gone against the Flying Circus! I've faced the Loezer Circus! I been up against the Archies—in a Nieuwpoort, no less! Hell! My nerves are cured! I've got four victories! My nerves are fine!"

"Go pick potatoes."

Jack Burton knew the company he was in. In the tent he kept his own counsel. At night he closed his eyes and dreamed of silvery skies, of Spads, of empty air on every side.

The other newcomer was more down to earth.

"Where you from," Jud Taylor asked.

"Cook County Jail," Swede Anderson said.

"Before that."

"City Jail, Ashtabula."

"Before that."

"Oneida County Jail, Utica."

"Well! Life does go on! Welcome to the U.S. Military Prison and Disciplinary Barracks. I'm sure you'll feel right at home."

Swede Anderson was a lean, fair-skinned man with sandy hair and a boyish face any mother would gladly clasp to her bosom. Many had. His biceps were even bigger than Covelli's.

"I never had no one to look after me, so I look after myself. Do a damn fine job, too. I worked on farms all over this country."

"So did I," Covelli said.

"Worked in factories too."

"So did I," Covelli said.

"Never lost a fight in my life."

Covelli had no answer. Swede Anderson waited a moment, then continued. "I'll take the farm over the factory any day. As for the war, no thanks, brother. It's a businessman's war. It's the bosses who are running things. Take it from me. Why should we get shot to preserve the lovely state of affairs we now enjoy?"

"You refused to serve," Jud Taylor said.

Swede Anderson smiled.

"How long did you get," Jud Taylor asked.

"They gave me life. But I'll outlast 'em. Just you watch."

"You a Wob?" Covelli said.

"Absolutely." Swede Anderson winked at Jack Burton.

The October nights were cold. Overhead, the stars had changed. Orion the hunter now looked down on Leavenworth. The prisoners in the yard had not yet been moved indoors to the barracks.

"What are your dreams," Jud Taylor asked one evening when the night was still.

"I got no dreams," Jack Burton said quickly.

"You mean dreams," Covelli asked.

"Yes, of course. Dreams."

"I ain't stupid. I sure ain't gonna tell you her name," Covelli said. "But she's about five foot two, eyes of blue, hair as black as night. And she's got a pair of knockers on her that could call the cows home from the next county!"

Everybody except Jacob laughed.

"I mean real dreams, of course. But not that kind, Covelli. I mean dreams for yourself. Dreams for your country and what you hope it will be. I mean dreams that help you along here, and keep you going, keep you up instead of down."

"Dreaming about Helen Louisa keeps me up, all right," Covelli said.

Everyone laughed again, except Jacob Decker.

"Freedom," Covelli said suddenly.

"That's all?"

"That's enough, ain't it? Freedom for all. No more bosses. Maybe some day they'll let us go. That's what I want."

"Daniel?" Jud Taylor said.

"South Hill is my dream."

"Now what in the hell is *that?*" Jack Burton laughed.

Covelli swung himself up to a sitting position and glared across the tent. "Maybe it's freedom to him, wise guy. You got no place to go home to?"

"I'll gladly tell you boys what I dream about," Swede Anderson said. "A fair day's pay for a day's work, with time out for lunch. That's what I'd like to see. What a farmer don't sell, he feeds to the pigs. What the pigs don't eat, he feeds to the dogs. What the dogs won't touch, he feeds to the chickens. The working stiffs get the rest. I'm for changing that. I'm with Covelli, I suppose. I dream of an eight-hour day when I get out, that's what. One big union. Let the bosses eat garbage."

"As for myself," Jud Taylor said, "my dreams tend to revolve about the notion of an equitable society and the evenhanded administration of justice for all—"

"I guessed as much," Covelli said.

"I think the state is the greatest single engine of oppression going. But I'm not like you, Covelli. I tend to think we need it. We need each other. Without the state, individuals wouldn't exist. We'd be nothing but animals. It's a paradox. You boys know what a paradox is? Generally speaking, a paradox is composed of any contrary conclusions, both of which are—"

"Animals are okay," Covelli said. "I've known a lot of fine animals in my time. No animal ever sent me to prison for standing up for what I believe in."

The tent fell silent.

"Jake?" Jud Taylor said. "What goes on in that big curly head of yours? Besides devotions, of course, in which I hope we're all included?"

Jacob stared at the ceiling of the tent. No one expected him to speak. "I tink of bacon and eggs," he said slowly. "I tink of buttered carrots. I tream of cherries and plums, baked beans, rice in sweet milk. Ach! I tink of sauerkraut and parsnips. I tink of pancakes with cheese and celery, which makes my mouth water. I tink of creamed corn. I tell you! I tink of sweet pickles. I tink of buttered beets. I tink of big rice pudding with the nutmegs! I tream of peaches. I tink all the time of *schuten krafen*. I tink of bread crumbs and onions fried in butter. I tream of stewed mutton with the horseradish. I tink of noodled soup. Bread and cheese I got in plenty. I tell you! I tream of milk and honey!"

There was a moment of stunned silence. Then everyone began to laugh.

Jacob looked at them with wide, glistening eyes. He swung his feet to the floor and sat up on the edge of his cot. Then he too began to laugh—a deep booming laugh that caught all of them by surprise. It was a laugh so hearty that it made their own seem feeble. Laughter rocked the tent. Jake laughed so hard his sides ached. Some boys in a nearby tent began to laugh as well. This made Daniel and the others laugh even harder. In the darkness they couldn't see the tears streaming down Jacob's cheeks.

"I tell you! I tream of milk and honey!"

The next morning he refused to work. He was taken from the line and marched across the yard to the dark angle between the fifth and sixth wings. This time there was no joking among the guards and yard officers who gathered around him. He was ordered to salute an officer. He refused. He was ordered to put on a military uniform. Jacob stood at attention, staring straight ahead, and did not speak. He refused to move. An officer called for a burlap sack. Jacob didn't budge.

They had to carry him downstairs to the hole.

"How long?" Daniel said, out in the potato fields.

"Long enough," Covelli grunted.

"You don't think he'll make it?"

"Not him. The poor bastard."

"But you made it, Covelli."

Covelli stood up and massaged his lower back. Across the way, Jud Taylor and the two newcomers were working on adjoining rows with another gang. Behind them loomed the gray walls of the prison. Daniel began digging with his fingers, dislodging more potatoes.

"He's stronger than all of us, Covelli. He's got a strong faith. He knows his mind."

"That's what I mean," Covelli said.

Word spread quickly. The prisoners talked in twos and threes in the fields, then in larger numbers while waiting in line for their supper. Some called for a general strike, but found few takers. Some called for staying clear out of it. A socialist from Cleveland called for a meeting in the seventh wing, where the prisoners were occasionally allowed to move freely between their cells.

"We've had more than enough," someone said.

"We're worse than dirt," said another.

"We got no chance at all," said a third.

"Let's not give up hope," Daniel said. "We can't lose hope."

"Hope of what," someone asked.

"You boys know what the Frenchies call *sabot*," Swede Anderson asked.

"I got no dream. None at all. I'm much too smart for that. Count me out," said Jack Burton.

The talk continued even after the prisoners were returned to their tents.

"We're all one, ain't we?" Daniel said. "If we don't stand up, then what's the use? It ain't worth it if we don't stand up for one another."

"Not me, not me."

"But if we all stand up together for what we feel?"

"I'm just a regular soldier boy, stuck in here with you goonies. You can count on one thing. Count me out."

"We need a fighter," Jud Taylor said. "Someone to stand up cool and steady to the commandant."

"You're the smartest one of all," Covelli said. "I suggest you be the one to stand up to the commandant, cool and steady. Eh?"

"Brains ain't necessarily brave, Covelli," someone pointed out.

"You're right about that. I fought a guy in Philly, was a teacher. A teacher by day, a pug on Saturday afternoons."

"Did you lose," Swede Anderson asked.

"I had him scared. Hell, I could see it in his eyes. He was real smart, but down inside I had him on the run."

"Then Taylor ain't the one. Don't trust people with a superfluity of brains—no offense, of course."

"I'll draw up the petition," Jud Taylor quickly offered.

"Talk to the others. You'll see they feel the same. We need a fighter. Someone who's at his best when his back's against the wall." He purposely did not look at Covelli. "I tend to think Daniel's right. The quiet one is right, as usual. If we cast aside our differences, if we stand together—"

"You mean me," Covelli asked.

"This could spread," the commandant said, pacing in his office. "I don't like the looks of it."

"There's room for all," his aide replied. He smiled reassuringly and reached for one of the commandant's good cigars.

The commandant stared at him.

"No, there isn't. Not for all."

That evening the tents in the yard were ordered struck. Several companies of soldiers arrived from the military reservation. They carried full packs and rifles. All the prisoners were moved inside the barracks, behind bars.

Covelli was elected to carry the word to the commandant. He stood in the commandant's office somewhat nervously, near the door, with his back against the wall. The commandant held the petition in his hand. It had been signed by thirty-one prisoners, none of them soldiers.

"All objectors," the aide observed.

"Less than ten percent," the commandant said. "Ten percent malcontents, the remainder being satisfied with the progressive administration of this facility."

"Some of them names just can't be true," the aide whispered, leaning over the commandant's shoulder. "Porky. Windy. Bones. Shorty. They're just nicknames. Or made up."

The commandant smiled at Covelli. "Even within that ten percent, not all are so convinced of their cause as to sign their true names."

Covelli shifted his weight from one foot to the other. "It speaks for all, no matter how many names."

The commandant looked over the list of grievances. "This is all you boys want?" he said. "More tobacco? An end to exercise in the yard? Improvement in the service of mail?" He raised an eyebrow. "The mail service is highly efficient. I've received no complaints to speak of. You want an end to what you care to call beatings and abuse? Force is a necessary evil among a population such as this, sir. No more manacles? What is this? No more manacles for murderers and thieves, and men who have betrayed their country's cause? Be realistic." The commandant scanned the rest of the list. "You want better food? Go to Paris. You want this man Decker removed from solitary confinement—"

"It's against his religion," Covelli said.

"Prison is against his religion?"

"War is."

"What is *your* religion?"

"I ain't got one. What's yours?"

The commandant shrugged. "All you want is pie in the sky. I suppose you would also like us to remove the bars throughout?"

"We want someone here from the War Department to see for himself," Covelli said.

The commandant turned to his aide. "How many men have refused to work and been taken to solitary?"

"Only one to solitary, sir. In all, three have refused to work. Two cousins of this man Decker tried to join him this morning."

"They weren't taken to solitary? I want them in solitary."

"They required some attention, sir, and were taken to the hospital."

The commandant was silent. He cupped his chin in his hand and stared at Covelli.

"What's your name?"

"Joseph Marie Covelli."

"You're Italian?"

"American."

"How much education have you had, Joseph?"

"Fourth grade. The rest I did on my own. How about you?"

The commandant was taken aback. "West Point," he finally said. "I learned enough there to know that the War Department is quite busy. Far too busy to bother with a few misguided slackers who refuse to serve, and who refuse even to work when confined. I'm afraid that's quite out of the question—"

"It ain't just Jake. It's all. I'm here to say we all feel the same. I'm speaking for all, because we're all one." Covelli clenched his fists. "It ain't you, I'm sure. This ain't against you, I'm instructed to say. It's against the whole stinking system. We want someone from the War Department here to see for himself."

The commandant sighed aloud. "You've got fortitude, Covelli. But not much judgment. That can be remedied. With a little training you could make a damn fine soldier. You could stand tall for your country. It falls within my limited powers to offer you an opportunity to enlist in the regular Army of the United States. Or, if your principles forbid, the Medical Corps or the Engineer's Corps—"

"To hell with that," Covelli blurted. "It's your war, you fight it. I'm an anarchist. I'm a free man. How come you ain't over there?"

The commandant ignored him. He strolled over to the window and stared out into the empty yard. There were squares of dead grass where the tents had stood, as though the prisoners had leached the life out of the earth.

"Dagos," the commandant said under his breath.

"I'm an American too," Covelli said loudly. "So I only went to fourth grade. What of it? I can still think for myself. You know what I think? It's all bullshit. It's all goddamn bosses telling you what to do!"

The commandant looked across the room at his aide. "You see the problem? Too many foreigners. That's the problem. They come here from everywhere. They have no allegiance at all. Take this man back to the barracks—"

"You won't do nothing?"

"I don't mean to the hospital. I mean to the barracks," the commandant emphasized.

"This means you won't do nothing? You'll just stand there and you won't do nothing?"

"You don't speak for all, Covelli," the commandant said. The aide opened the door and beckoned Covelli through, keeping a safe distance.

"Then there ain't no hope," Daniel said when Covelli returned.

"I tried my best," Covelli said.

Daniel stood at the door to their cell on the third floor of the seventh wing. Swede Anderson and Jack Burton occupied the two bunks. Jud Taylor and Covelli sat on the floor against the rear wall.

"Not enough would stand up, Daniel," Jud Taylor said. "That's the whole story."

"Not for Jake. Not for each other. Not for themselves."

"Not me," Jack Burton said. "You boys are begging for trouble. I'm surprised they brought you back here, Covelli. Instead of downstairs."

Covelli had his head in his hands. He didn't stir.

"You never know what will bring men together," Jud Taylor said. "Self-interest keeps them apart. There's an anarchism of interests here, that's for sure. And a lack of fortitude."

"Speak for yourself," Covelli said softly. "I tried. I done my best."

"Nothing personal, Covelli. I'm sure you were cool and steady."

From where Daniel stood, the high window opposite the walkway in front of the cell gave a view only of the sky. "The mail don't even come through anymore," he said. "Never hear from the loved ones at home."

"There ain't no loved ones," said a boy in the next cell. "Not for the likes of us."

After a time Swede Anderson stirred. "She have a name?"
Daniel was silent.

Covelli finally answered. "Her name is Caroline. Stay out of it, red bird. Leave him alone."

The Kansas sky was gray and sullen. It stretched away uniformly to a horizon no one could see. But the color and the mood were reflected in Daniel's eyes.

13

Clouds streamed southward over Winchester. Shadows swept the countryside below. Strings of wild geese in sixes and sevens straggled on the wind.

The house at South Hill seemed desolate.

In a few short weeks the coat of summer paint had turned gray. The stone foundation showed cracks where the mortar had washed away. The sunflowers bloomed and were forgotten. A hard rain partially stripped the stalks of standing corn in the south field. The walking plow remained with an air of abandonment in the north field where Livia had left it. Who even spoke to Livia Hanson? The town whore, once, and a boy of feeble mind.

She saw him one chilly afternoon through the kitchen window. He stood in the side yard, with his head awkwardly cocked to one side as though listening for something in the earth, or in the wind. His black hair was long and matted. His eyes were anxious. He was inadequately dressed for the weather, wearing only a thin shirt and trousers.

Livia wiped her hands and stepped out onto the porch.

"Yes?" she said.

"They're gonna burn you out," the boy said ominously.

Livia opened the porch door and stepped down to the slab of stone at the foot of the stairs.

"You're Emmett Minor?"

He nodded vigorously in acknowledgment. "They're gonna burn you out, ma'am, house and all." He waved his arm at the house like a magician about to perform an illusion of very grand proportions.

"How do you know that?"

"I heard 'em say it. And I come to warn you." His face brightened. The wind blew Livia's skirts. Emmett Minor shivered, and rubbed his bare arms.

"How did you come here, Emmett?"

"Right through the fields, so as not to be seen," he said proudly.

Livia pressed her hand to her forehead. Beyond the boy in the yard she could see the stretch of fields, a patch of sky, the sailing clouds.

"Would you like some coffee, Emmett? To warm yourself? Or a slug of pie?"

"Well! I'm very much obliged, I'm sure."

He came forward cautiously.

A few minutes later what remained of the morning coffee was reheated. The pie was cut. Livia Hanson sat with Emmett Minor at the kitchen table. He was the first real company she had had—a boy of feeble mind.

"I seen you into town. To Hoover's," he said.

"I don't dare go to Hadley's, for his views."

"They're very strong. You're very right. He's amongst 'em."

"Bull Hadley is?"

"I heard him say it, ma'am. Him and others. They'll burn you out in their own good time."

"For what cause, Emmett?"

"You want me to say it?"

"Not if you don't wish to, Emmett."

He looked down at the table. He couldn't look her in the eye. "Don't like you, ma'am," he mumbled. "Don't like the way that one stands against all. You lost the mister on its account—not to knuckle under. It's just the way they feel—so strong." He looked up suddenly. "But I told the sheriff all the talk to burn you out. 'We shall see,' he said."

Livia's lips were drawn in a tight line.

"Sheriff Bonner? He shall see?"

"It's a very nice kitchen," Emmett Minor said.

He ate in silence, then asked for more coffee. Livia brewed another pot. She brought him one of Peter's heavy shirts and draped it over his shoulders. The shirt was large for him but he looked up at her with grateful eyes, like a dog unaccustomed to kindness. Livia suddenly felt lonely, more lonely than she ever felt while alone.

"Do you know Frisco Fritz?" he said.

"I do."

"A kindly man. Do you know Dr. Homer Armand Pratt?"

"I do."

"Kate Hoover's very nice."

"She can be, when she so desires."

"Do you miss the mister?"

"Yes, Emmett. I do."

"I saw it happen. The way he fought."

"You saw him fight?"

"Guy Martini and Joseph Henry Webb. He whipped 'em both."

"Is that so?" Livia said.

"You declare for the war or against," Emmett asked.

Livia was silent.

"Everyone's for or against," he added.

"I'm for the country, that it be strong and free. And have a place for boys and men who are likewise."

Livia listened to her own voice. It sounded strange, unexercised. All the silence; all the strain of seeing right from wrong, and carrying on alone; all the necessary trips into town, the turning heads, the sullen stares—all this bore down on her. She and Emmett Minor had this much in common: no one to talk to, no one to speak of true feelings with.

"If you should need me, I can help," Emmett said suddenly. "Can't do much, but I can lift." He had blueberry sauce at the corners of his wide mouth.

That evening Doc Pratt and Sheriff Bonner occupied a bench next to Jack Hurley's saloon.

"Delivered a baby with two heads," Doc Pratt announced. "To a farm wife out near Camp Merrill."

"Two heads?" the sheriff said.

"One very badly formed, as though it were the stump of a leg or an arm."

"I heard of it in calves."

"This was a human baby."

"It didn't live?"

"Born dead," Doc Pratt replied. "A hope that turned out bad." He looked across the street at Hadley's store. The store was closed but the lights were on in back, where Bull Hadley sat around the warming stove with some of his cronies.

"Town's held together with silence," Sheriff Bonner said.

"It's held together, save but one."

"I give her credit," Sheriff Bonner said after a time.

Doc Pratt stared into the night. He was silent.

"It ain't easy what she's had to do. Nor what she's up against," Sheriff Bonner added. "The town just won't let go. So I give her credit where it's due. Seen her plowing a while back. I've half a mind to help her out, should I find the time."

"All on account of conscience," Doc Pratt said.

Sheriff Bonner bristled. "I'm not without a conscience," he declared, somewhat sharply.

"You misunderstand, sir."

Across the street, Bull Hadley placed his black cigar between the upraised legs of the sea nymph in his ashtray and rubbed it gently back and forth. "Look at it however you want," he said. "Been a very good year for all."

"Wheat's been very fine," one of his cronies said.

"Price keeps going higher," said another.

"Highest price ever known."

"Good for business, if nothing else."

"You ain't for it," Bull Hadley asked.

"Hell, yes! I'm for it! I sure am that! I'm a four-minute man, ain't I?"

"One of the best. Keeps our spirits high," Bull Hadley said.

There was a new hired hand at Old Man Curtis's farm. His name was Thomas Riley. He wore white shirts with bands around his arms when he wasn't working. He had a handsome face, dark eyes full of the devil, and a dark mustache. He knew more card tricks than anyone west of Wichita.

"You know anything about temptation," Old Man Curtis asked Carrie one day.

"I'm tempted to say no."

"That fellow Riley's a hard worker. On the other hand, stay away from him."

When Thomas Riley drove Carrie into town on the wagon, he reached down and drew her up to the wagon seat by putting his arm around her waist.

Kate Hoover stared at him one day in town. He stared back from the wagon seat.

"Exempted as a married man, ma'am," he declared, without being asked.

Kate Hoover continued to stare.

"The wife stayed behind in Wichita," he added. He smiled and touched the brim of his straw hat.

"I hope she will join you," Kate Hoover said dryly.

"My hope as well. But in this toiling life, not all our hopes are realized."

His eyes had left Kate Hoover's. He was watching Carrie Curtis walk from Hadley's store with a package of stationery securely wrapped. She looked fresh and beautiful.

Thomas Riley reached down and swung her up onto the wagon seat next to him. His hand lingered at her waist.

Some time later, Michael Carr moved skillfully through the steamy shower room prison. He brushed up against Daniel. "She loves you, is what she says, and will wait for you forever."

"Forever?"

But Michael Carr was gone.

Jamie Hanson raced toward home as fast as his legs could carry him. He tried to keep up with the racing shadows that swept down the town road. His legs flew. His arms flew. His face was radiant. At the foot of the lane leading up to South Hill he shifted his schoolbook from one hand to the other. He gulped the cold afternoon air. Then he lowered his head and dashed up the lane toward the house.

Livia heard him coming.

The porch door banged as he burst into the kitchen: "John Curtis!"

Livia was startled.

"What of him?"

"Coming home!"

"Oh, my God!"

Jamie gasped for breath. His shirttails were pulled out from his trousers. One of his suspenders had fallen to his hip. The elastic cuffs of his knickers slipped down. He reached for the wall to steady himself.

"They're letting him go from the war!" he finally said. "They're giving a hero's welcome! Band and all!" He threw his arms out and leaped into the air. His hair flew. Livia could feel her heart beating wildly.

"John Curtis. After all this time," she said softly.

They sat together at the table in the kitchen. "I want to be in it, Ma. I *have* to be," Jamie said. "It's a hero's welcome on the seven-ten tonight!" His face beamed.

"From whom did you hear?"

"The horse's mouth, I'll have you know!"

"And who was the horse, may I ask?"

"William O. Waters, stationmaster. I saw him at the depot talking with some others, and strolled on by. Cool as a cucumber, like you've said, as though I couldn't care a hang for what they were saying! It was William O. Waters himself who said 'a hero's welcome'!"

"And who were the others, if I may ask?"

"It was Webb and Briggs and Mr. Hoover, from Hoover's store. Mr. Simon Turner did most of the talking."

"Mr. Simon Turner, did you say?"

"It's our own John Curtis, Ma."

Livia pushed herself away from the table with trembling hands.

Shortly before seven o'clock that evening Jamie Hanson sat high in the old warehouse adjoining the tracks and depot. He had scrambled up the side and followed wooden ladders to the very top, where he sat beneath the overhanging eave with a fine view of all. The November air was chill. Jamie felt like a bird flying high and free in the Kansas air, with a heart about to burst from happiness. Far below, Sheriff Abel Bonner looked like a midget. He stood with his burly arms folded, talking with Mr. Bull Hadley. Bud Curtis moved briskly through the crowd, trailing his hand from one outstretched palm to another. His black felt hat was pulled low over his eyes, so as not to betray his joy. Wagons crowded the street. People stood in groups of two and three, talking quietly with each other in the evening light. At the base of the warehouse, almost directly beneath Jamie's roost, Frisco Fritz stood at strict attention with four members of the Winchester band—all he could enlist on such short notice. Old Man Curtis and his wife Millie and Carrie had moved their wagon to the center of the crowd, near the edge of the tracks. They sat as still as death, so great was their own happiness.

William O. Waters was dressed in a black suit with white cuffs. He walked stiffly back and forth along the track bed, peering north. "It's late, folks. Sorry to say. It's late, folks."

The band struck up a tune. Men reached automatically for their hats. When the tune was over, people began to laugh and talk more freely. Now and then they clapped each other on the back, and stamped their feet. The sky was like a fading prairie rose. By gradual degrees it turned the darkest blue. Jamie began to grown cold, perched so high above the earth.

The band struck up another tune.

William O. Waters disappeared into the depot.

Bud Curtis separated himself from the crowd below and headed up the street toward Mary Lane's saloon with Thomas Riley, the hired hand. Riley carried his straw hat in his hand. Bud dragged his bad leg.

"He's on his way! He's on his way," William Waters cried out when he emerged from the depot. He stalked up and down, stiff-legged, talking to no one. Jamie squirmed. Old Man Curtis and his wife and daughter didn't move. It was nearly twenty minutes more before the mournful whistle of the locomotive drifted across the prairie from the north.

The crowd grew still.

Jamie twisted around on the rafter, peering up the street for Bud Curtis, but the street was empty. In the opposite direction he could see the wobbling lights of the locomotive more than a mile away, coming down toward town. Jamie's heart started to trip with anticipation. Soon Mr. Waters went up and down the platform encouraging people to move back from the tracks. The train came in behind him, moving slowly past the crowd. The engineer leaned from the window of his cab, looking back. He pulled only three cars. The last of them stopped directly in front of Old Man Curtis's wagon.

Carrie Curtis reached up and removed her hat. Jamie inched forward. Light seeped from around the drawn green shades of the car's windows. The door to the car opened hesitantly and a soldier in uniform peered out. A low murmur arose from the crowd, and the soldier stepped quickly back inside.

"Okay? Okay?" Frisco Fritz was saying down below.

Someone nodded.

Frisco Fritz brought down his baton with a flourish. The band struck up a mighty hymn. The door on the car opened once again, and two strong soldiers started backwards down the steps, carrying one end of the pine coffin.

Carrie Curtis buried her face in her hands.

High above her, Jamie Hanson's knuckles had turned white. He held onto the rafter with all his might.

By the time he finally reached the ground, people were moving away. They were dark forms in the night, most of them hurrying to Mary Lane's or Hurley's. Jamie stumbled along with them.

"What was it?" someone said.

"Influenza, is what I heard."

"Well, he's just as dead, ain't he? Just as dead as if he caught a bullet from a Hun."

"Died a hero, of influenza. Served his country well, I would suppose."

Old Man Curtis's wagon was far down the town road on its way home. A few people lingered at the depot, where Frisco Fritz and the band struck up another verse of "America the Beautiful"—all the more stirring for the smallness of their numbers. Someone started to sing the words, alone at first, then joined by others. The music wafted through the town. It embraced the good people of Winchester and rose upward in the darkness toward the stars, like a prayer yet to be answered.

The stars still flew westward on the wind.

They were cold and silent.

"I am absolutely without feeling," Carrie Curtis said. She leaned faintly against the doorway to John's room, looking at his meager possessions. Her mother stood behind her.

"You will regain it. The feeling will come."

A short time later the little prairie lane that led off the town road was crowded with automobiles and wagons parked haphazardly at every angle. The old iron gate marked the entrance to Kansas Rest Cemetery.

The sky was filled with long, leaden breakers rolling down upon the Kansas prairie. The prairie itself overflowed with people, nearly all the town of Winchester and some from far beyond. A contingent of soldiers from Camp Merrill, smartly dressed, stood at attention part way up the rise. They faced the robed choir of the Pearl City Faith Church. All ten members of the Winchester marching band stood beside the choir. Frisco Fritz held his hands tightly behind his back. The clarinetist stared at them.

The crowd formed an aisle several people deep through which Old Man Curtis walked with his wife and daughter. His head was bowed, his rounded shoulders bent. His step was slow. Millie Curtis held his arm. Carrie walked at her mother's side.

It was Carrie, searching the faces of the mourners, who first saw Livia Hanson.

She tugged at her mother's sleeve. Millie turned around, and her eyes met Livia's. She stepped tentatively toward the crowd. Livia stepped forward. They met halfway, clasping each other in a tight embrace.

"Oh Millie!"

"Oh Livvie! Our hopes are nothing!"

"I feel like he's my own! He's like my own!"

"It must be bringing us nearer to something we don't know!"

"Oh Millie!"

"Oh Livvie! O Livvie!"

They separated as quickly as they had embraced. Old Man Curtis had walked on a few paces before stopping. He didn't turn around. When Millie rejoined him, the procession continued up the rise. Livia sank back into the crowd.

"We cling to our hopes, like flowers that fade in our arms," the woman next to her whispered. "It is my prayer this war can soon be brought to a conclusion. And friends can once again be friends."

Livia stared blindly ahead, blinking the tears from her eyes. Only after several moments did she realize that Kate Hoover was addressing these remarks to her.

Jack Burton was the first to hear. He was, after all, an aviator. His ears were attuned to the future, to the throaty roar of engines and their endless changes, as momentous in their way as cathedral bells. What he heard was the peal of bells, the rise and fall of distant sirens. He rose quietly from his blanket on the floor. He paced about the cell, then stationed himself at the door. His fingers—accustomed to smooth leather, seasoned wood, finished metal, taut canvas—caressed the cold bars.

Jud Taylor suddenly closed his book. He listened.

"It's over," he announced.

Throughout the Disciplinary Barracks, prisoners rushed to the doors of their cells. They stood around the periphery of the cell block staring at the dark windows. Down in the yard officers and guards stepped out of doorways and looked up at the sky.

They looked at each other, dumbstruck. The sirens grew louder. Now and then a Roman candle or a flare appeared over the rooftops in the direction of town.

"The war is over," Jud Taylor said. He looked at Daniel. "It's over." He looked at Covelli. "The war is over!"

"For some," Covelli said.

The silence in the cell blocks slowly gave away. Hands wrapped tightly around the bars, men stood at the cell doors and shook them back and forth against the latches. The din grew and grew, until it was like thunder rolling through their hearts.

All across Kansas the telegraph chattered. Men burst out of doors, looking up into the night. Men who had never fought cried victory.

On a side street in Kansas City a peanut vendor's stand was overturned because it bore no flag. A mob set the stand afire while the vendor backed down the street in darkness, gesturing wildly. He spoke no English except "Tank you," which he said over and over. Near Topeka flames consumed a Mennonite church. "An act of God," the fire marshal said. "Helpless to do a thing." Elsewhere church doors bloomed with bullet holes. In Garden City the town's only tailor was rousted out of bed to witness the destruction of his store. His name was Stein. He'd written more than three hundred letters to newspaper editors in opposition to the war. Six had been published. In a town called Coffeyville a black woman named Rosabelle listened to the shouts and whistles on the street. She looked at Mr. Rabbit, and she looked at Mr. Dog. "Over at last, honeys. The war's over at last." She took a bottle from the fist of the man who lay next to her in bed, and lifted it to her lips.

Men everywhere were in masks or sheets or on the run. Torches were held high in the air. Children raced down the street with faces lifted skyward, hair flying, arms outspread like airplanes.

What happened in Kansas happened all across America. The low-slung wires sang victory.

Old Man Curtis rested his head on the back of his overstuffed chair. The parlor was dark. His jaw was slack, his mouth wide open. His eyes stared upward. He saw nothing—not the extent of his wheat fields, nor the vigor of his cattle. He saw only darkness and a proud treasure snatched away. Millie sat across from him. Her hands were folded gently in her lap. Her eyes were closed.

Bud Curtis reached for his hat.

From Winchester the mob headed north toward Prairie Flower. They numbered seven automobiles, more than twenty men. They carried torches, gasoline, greasy rags, rocks, rifles. They announced the end of the war in plain English to the families of several German families north of town. They left behind the pungent scent of smoke and gunpowder. Then they headed east along the county road, laughing and singing, following its straight fences even deeper into darkness. The headlamps of the automobiles made little yellow pinpricks in the Kansas night. The empty bottles went over the sides of the cars.

The cars turned south.

"Ma?"

"What?"

"Are you awake?"

"Yes. Come here, Jamie."

"There's men outside, Ma."

His voice was small and frightened.

Livia opened her eyes with a start. Pale light rode the bedroom wall in waves. Jamie stood in the doorway. For a moment she thought it was Daniel. Or Peter. All began to slip away.

"Get your shoes on," she ordered.

"They're on. They're all around the house, Ma. I seen some in back—"

"Go look. Go look again!"

Suddenly she was up and dressed. Her heart pounded. She cinched her belt a little too tightly, and brushed the hair back from her eyes. She hurried through the house toward the porch. At the parlor door she wiped her hands nervously on her dress.

The men were gathered in the yard like ghosts, masked by sheets and pillowcases. Black and yellow flames leaped from their torches. Behind them Livia saw their automobiles parked along the town road, with some parked in the lane.

"I see her," someone shouted. "There she is!"

"Come on down," another voice boomed.

She turned to Jamie. "Get your father's gun." He turned and ran through the darkened house. The men in the yard milled about. Overhead was darkness, coming down to meet the flames.

"The war is over, Livia! Near caught us by surprise!"

"Get off that porch! We mean no harm to you!"

"Come on down," someone shouted.

Two or three figures broke from the others and ran for the back of the house. Livia pushed open the screen door and stepped down. Her hand waved behind her back, until Jamie put the rifle into it.

"It ain't loaded," Jamie whispered.

"Get away," Livia shouted. "You leave this place alone!" Her voice surprised her by its strength.

"Ain't loaded, Ma," came the whisper behind her.

From the back of the house came the sound of breaking glass and shouting men. Livia could hear Old Don begin to pound his hooves against the stall. The wavering gun barrel swept the yard but no one moved.

"War's over, Livia!"

"Where's that young one? Get him down!"

"Get on away," Livia cried again. "You all get home! The sheriff's on his way!"

There was a crash in the kitchen, then another in the parlor. Jamie dashed down the porch stairs onto the lawn as the gang of men suddenly broke and ran for the cars. Torches went sailing into the night toward the house. Livia didn't move.

Flames swept through the house behind her.

Far across Kansas, in the Disciplinary Barracks, a guard strolled along the edges of a cell block in the seventh wing. "That's a false alarm, boys! The war ain't over yet. Go on to sleep like good boys," he shouted. "That there's a false alarm! Go on to sleep! The war ain't over yet. . . ."

Daniel listened to the guard's voice trail away.

Hours later, Livia still stood in the south field. The brilliant light pinned her against the darkness. Jamie nestled in her skirts, wide-eyed. She held her husband's empty rifle in her hand.

Great plumes and pinwheels of fire reached toward the morning stars.

14

The armistice was signed four days later.

Livia had taken rooms in town over the shop of Mr. Frisco Fritz. She came straight to his place from the prairie and woke him from a restless sleep. He noticed her stately bearing and the resolution that was so plain in her eyes. To others he mentioned none of this.

"I'm broke. I'm busted. I need the money," he told everyone. "Music pays in joy and balm for broken hearts. I need some do-re-mi." Then he laughed his nervous little laugh.

"We like you, Fritz," everyone answered. "You're okay, Fritz. We know your heart's in the right place. By God, we understand."

"Just taking in a stray," some said. "Why, hell, I'd do the same myself—if forced."

"What's she paying," others asked.

"Once a night? Twice a night?"

"Twice a night and once at noon!"

"A stick like her? All skin and bones?"

"They're the ones as work the hardest."

"A weasel like that Frisco Fritz?"

The town talked all right. Someone even said, "Now there's

a hard thing for a woman to do, ain't it? She lost her husband. Lost her boy, who was a good boy all in all, although I disagree. Lost everything in that fire, yet comes right in to make a way for herself. And with that young one yet to raise. I give her credit where it's due."

Another said, "I don't mind saying, I prayed the war would soon be brought to a conclusion. It brought too much death and suffering to us all. Now it's done. I'm glad it is. Friends can once again be friends. In due time, of course."

Livia was overcome with calmness.

"I'll give you bedclothes and some plates. Plates from Dresden—a lovely city, with linden trees. I'll stake you to a month. Maybe two," Frisco Fritz said. "On the grounds of humanity, you understand. This is between you and me, Livia. No one else."

"But how will I repay?"

"What can you do," he asked.

"I can cook and I can sew. I can hoe and I can hammer. I can raise up kids, which is out of the question."

"Your time will come, a woman like you." He looked at her and saw everything he was not.

The insurance adjustor came up from Pearl City and poked about the ruins.

"It ain't just one that did it, it's all," Bull Hadley explained, deftly shifting a cigar from one corner of his mouth to the other. "It's quite impossible to indict. I checked the statutes."

"The policy has lapsed," the insurance adjustor said.

"That suits me fine," Bull Hadley said.

Carrie Curtis looked at her mother with red-rimmed eyes. "I been over to see it. There's nothing left. Just ruins and desolation, nearly level to the ground."

"Stay away," said Old Man Curtis.

"She could have come here," Millie said. "I wish she had. Why didn't she?"

"She's proud, is why," Carrie answered. "She's got more

spunk than any Curtis. It's a free country when all is said and done, save for those as have the courage to suffer their beliefs."

"Give it up, daughter. Cast him out."

"Daniel went to war as sure as John did!"

"It's time you growed up."

"I *am* grown up. You just can't see!"

"I see plenty well. I just don't know the workings of your heart, if you even have one. I've yet to see a tear for John."

"I am without feeling."

"Not entire," Curtis said. "You carry on about that boy—"

"I cried for John. I'll cry for who I wish, without your saying." Her gray eyes flashed.

"That Liv has courage," Millie said, hoping to change the subject. "and in great measure, to greet me as she did, before the entire town."

"It's her sorrow too, Mother. It's all our sorrow—"

"Stay away. Still goes for all."

The guard jangled his keys ceremoniously.

"Is that him? Number fifty-seven?"

"Yes," Michael Carr said.

"Hanson? You're wanted," said the guard. He unlocked the cell door. The bolt clanged open.

"We'll be wanting him back," someone said from within the cell.

"No fear of that. You'll get him." The guard laughed. He slammed the cell door and threw the bolt, then continued on his way around the cell block jangling his keys. Daniel and Michael Carr followed the walkway in the opposite direction.

"I've got some records that must be moved from storage. Statistics and such. I need a strong back and a willing hand. You naturally come to mind." Carr smiled. "There's something sublime about even the simplest mathematics and statistics, don't you think? The addition of one, the subtraction of one, the difference such an operation makes upon the whole?"

"You said the hole?"

Michael Carr's voice dropped to a whisper. "Jacob wants to see you one last time."

Daniel looked at him, alarmed.

"Still refuses food," Carr said grimly. "More than a week now."

Since Jacob Decker went into the hole, Michael Carr had carried occasional reports of his amazing fortitude to the other inmates. He made it his business to pass by the subbasement cells at least daily on one pretext or another. "He bears up well, considering the circumstance. Hangs from the manacles ten hours per day in lieu of work, and refuses to speak. The pain must be thrilling. He may yet lead the slaves." None understood the allegiances of Michael Carr's heart. But now even he seemed to feel the ebb of hope.

The steps led downward by turns into the lower tiers of the seventh wing, and then into the basement and subbasement of the prison. The earthen walls were as cold as a grave.

"He asked for me?"

"Specifically," Carr said.

At the base of the stairs a well-lighted hallway stretched off to the right. At the far end a guard slumped behind a desk.

"Records," Michael Carr shouted down the hallway. His voice echoed, and was swallowed up by silence. The guard lifted one large hand and waved in acknowledgment. "His name is Simms," Carr said quietly to Daniel. "Slow-witted, but a beast. You'll have to hurry." He opened a heavy iron door, disclosing another corridor. This one was shorter and poorly illumined by a single bulb. Water seeped from the walls, trickling across the floor.

Daniel followed Michael Carr past several dark and empty cells. They stopped in the middle of the corridor, beneath the light.

Peter Knels and Joseph Wurz were mere shadows in the cells to either side. They hung by manacles with their heads pitched awkwardly at an angle. They didn't move. Jacob was suspended in the cell between them. Two short links of heavy chain connected the irons on his wrists to bolts pounded into the ceiling. His arms were crossed above his head. His prison shirt was soaked with sweat despite the chill. It clung to the wasted knots of bone and muscle that once made up the fortress of his heart. His pants were dark with piss and sweat. His feet did not touch the floor.

"Jake! It's Michael Carr. I told you miracles were quite beyond me, yet here I have one—Hanson. Can you hear?"

"I tink so—"

"It's me, Jake!" Daniel gripped the bars and stared at Jacob's shaggy face. Decker's eyes glowed like an animal's, reflecting the sickly illumination of the light bulb overhead.

"Old Jacob, old and weak . . . Knels Prairie . . . do you remember . . ."

"I do!"

"Please to tell him, Daniel . . . I take his hand . . . I wait for him in heaven, and not to be afraid—"

Jacob's chest heaved. His mouth trembled. His eyes were focused on something far away.

"I will!"

"He's a goddamn horse, ain't he?" came a voice behind them. Daniel turned around to face the guard, who had padded down the hall and into the hole. "Refused supper," the guard said good-naturedly. "And I in turn refused to take him down. A horse like him? Without assistance? These other boys have the right idea. They go unconscious soon as they get strung up. Ten minutes is all they take. Not this one! He's a side of beef, ain't he? Keeps them damn eyes open all the time. Don't look! He'll witch you sure as hell." The guard grinned.

Michael Carr moved forward, but Daniel pushed him out of the way. His fist caught the guard square in the face.

"Good Christ." Carr whispered.
Daniel's brown eyes widened.
The guard lay at their feet without moving.

Michael Carr waved from the doorway ahead. Daniel stepped from the shadows and staggered toward him. Harold Simms was slung over his back like a sack of potatoes. The guard's hands tapped at the back of Daniel's legs. Michael Carr pushed the door open. "Dump him!"

Daniel bent forward. Simms slid off his shoulders into the yellow mud of the prison yard. A cold rain was falling. A searchlight methodically swept the yard.

Carr quickly pulled the door shut.

"What of Simms?"

"They'll find him soon enough. Don't worry."

"And the records?"

"It's taken care of. I moved them myself this afternoon. Don't worry."

They headed quickly up the hall.

"What of Jacob?"

"Try to keep your voice low," Michael Carr advised. "If we're stopped, try to stay calm. Let me do the talking. Okay?"

"You're always helping someone, aren't you, Daniel?" Otis Judson Taylor asked when Daniel returned to the cell. "You're unable to prevent it. If there were more of you about, perhaps there'd be no need for war."

"I wouldn't help that little faggot *too* much," Jack Burton said. "I don't like the looks of him."

"He serves a purpose," Covelli said.

"So do worms," Burton said. "What is it?"

"Both feed upon the dead," Swede Anderson said cheerfully.

Daniel stood at the door of the cell. Gusts of wind and rain slapped against the high window opposite. Covelli shuffled over to him.

"I noticed the knuckles on your hand," he said softly. "Stepped on by a soldier?"

"In a manner of speech."

"Same thing happened to me many times," Covelli whispered. "At the Quaker Club in Philly. Keep moving the fingers."

Neither looked at the other.

"I don't know, Covelli. The war is over. Yet the war goes on within us."

Lights burned late in the commandant's office. The commandant wore two sweaters and his heavy Army overcoat. The radiator had not been properly repaired. The aide leaned against the wall in his slicker.

"He's been taken into town," the commandant asked.

"Through this lousy rain. It took forever. But the facilities are more suited."

"Where was he found?"

"Between the first and second wings, in the yard."

"He left his post?"

"It looks that way. The boys in the hole were still strung up. Should have come down at supper. My feeling is, Simms left his post before then and was jumped in the yard."

"How bad was he hurt?"

"Jaw and cheekbone, sir. Both fractured."

The commandant ran his fingers through his hair and stared at the scattered slips of statistics on his desk.

"Is he conscious?"

"Yes, sir. But he refuses to talk."

"Then he knows who did it."

"He must."

"And intends to take matters into his own hands."

"It looks that way. Unless—"

"Yes?"

"Unless a friend of his did it, or an enemy in the ranks, and he don't want to peach. It was always my plain suspicion that Hogan was done in by someone in the ranks. This may be the same."

The commandant considered this.

"I don't want him back," he said abruptly. "Pay his benefits. Give him a bonus. I want him terminated. We have things under excellent control here. We can't afford to lose it by allowing private action. We'll take care of it here. Understood?"

"Yes, sir. Understood."

"I want to know the name of the man who hit him, whether prisoner or guard or officer. Offer the usual blandishments. These men will be quite willing to talk."

"Yes, sir."

"They distrust each other. They pull in separate directions. That's the way we want it. It's the only way to manage such a large body of men."

"Yes, sir."

Even as the commandant spoke, some of the prisoners were being shifted on his orders from one part of the barracks to another. In this way the commandant hoped to break up established friendships and prevent the formation of seditious cabals.

The seventh wing was dark and quiet, except for the distant ring of a telephone. Daniel stood at the cell door. His right hand hung limply at his side, the fingers working slowly back and forth.

From overhead, someone shouted: "Burgandy! Is that you?"

The telephone stopped.

"Hallo-o-o, sweetie," a voice rang out, sweet and melodious. "This here's Burgandy! We in b-i-i-i-g trouble here tonight...."

By morning the rain had ceased. The inmates of the seventh wing tried to stand at attention in the yard.

A corporal paraded up and down before them.

"No need to tell you boys about the trouble," he declared. "We all got to live together, ain't that right? We're all God's children, givin' and takin' to get along. I been very understanding of you slackers, and all you good religious boys straight off from the farm, and even you proletariats who think your principles prevent you from war. Is there a man here who can't say I been understanding to a very large degree?" The prisoners shuffled their feet in the mud. Puddles reflected the pearl-gray sky. No one spoke. "And of course I will continue to be highly understanding of all," the corporal added. "But in order to do so, what I need this morning is some real solid information about who kicked the shit out of Harold Simms."

A murmur of nervous laughter swept up and down the line. Daniel didn't move.

"Here's my deal," the corporal said, slapping his hands together. "Someone saw it happen. Someone heard tell of it. Someone knows something, ain't that right? I would like for that someone to step forward and disclose himself. We will discuss in private. We will make a fine arrangement with a certain girl I know in town, my treat." He smiled broadly and looked them over. The prisoners stared at the ground. "If someone here is afraid to step forward because of the unpredictable nature of his fellow inmates, he will step forward in private. We will make the same arrangement, involving the same girl, who knows more tricks than you boys can imagine. Even you boys from the farm. A deal?"

Joseph Marie Covelli stepped forward.

Daniel stared at Covelli in disbelief. The corporal's eyes lighted up. This would be easier than he had thought.

"Yes, Covelli?" the corporal said, with an encouraging smile.

Covelli cleared his throat. "I did it, sir," he announced loudly.

The line shifted. Heads turned. The corporal's smile vanished.

"You did it?"

"Yes, sir," Covelli repeated. "I did it. I hit him."

Daniel struggled to stand at attention, but couldn't. He took two steps forward and stood next to Covelli.

"I did it," Daniel said. "Not Covelli! It was me."

"You *both* did it? You did it together?" The corporal frowned.

Down at the far end of the line, a skinny pacifist with spectacles stepped forward in the mud.

"*I* did it, sir!" he said. "And I'm damn glad I did."

The line of prisoners was no longer silent. Murmurs rippled up and down. Three boys stepped forward together.

"*We* did it, sir," one said. "Took all three of us, he's so big and ugly. We beat the shit out of the stinking bastard, as you said."

Prisoners began to step forward.

"I did it, sir!"

"It was me!"

"I did it!"

"Left hook! Right on the button! I did it, sir!"

"I did it! Happy to oblige!"

"I did it!"

"I did it!"

"I did it!"

Daniel's head swam. One by one, the prisoners stepped forward to shoulder the blame—even Jack Burton, who stood half a stride ahead of the others so he could be noticed. Burton's eyes burned with all the anger he'd kept within since Calais and St. Etienne. "Not them! Not them goonies," he shouted. "They couldn't hurt a fly! It was me! It's me who's the regular soldier. I been up against the Flying Circus. I been to France, have you? I'm for the war! I hit the lousy pacifist sonofabitch!"

The corporal had climbed atop the parade stand and was screaming back: "Dismissed! Dismissed! Back to your cells, you lousy bastards! Bible bangers! Crusaders! Bolsheviks! You stinking cowards! You goddamn yellow dogs! Dismissed!" His hands waved frantically toward the guardhouse.

The inmates stood shoulder to shoulder, chins up, chests out. They turned all at once, almost like soldiers, and crossed the dismal yard in small groups. Each boy's face was bright.

Covelli draped his arm over Daniel's shoulder.

"See what you started, lad," he asked quietly.

Daniel turned away. Tears filled his eyes. "It wasn't me. It was *you*. We *are* one, Covelli."

"When one man stands, more will follow," Covelli said.

The lesson of the seventh wing was not lost on the other prisoners. There was less quarreling. Boys who had been silent began to laugh and talk of home. One day, when it started to snow, prisoners in a work gang from the third wing threw down their picks and shovels. Some took shelter beneath a cottonwood, others in the protective cover of the prison wall. They spent the rest of the day stamping their feet in the snow and swapping stories about a certain girl in Kalamazoo. The guards stood under another tree and lighted cigars.

"They're refusing to work."

"It's only momentary. Overlook it."

"It's their goose being cooked. Leave 'em be."

"The war's over, ain't it?"

"It's mighty cold, is what it is!"

"Got a bottle on you?"

The mercury continued to fall. The boilers were fired night and day. The wind carried the snow away, but left a crust of ice in the water tanks about the yard. Dead leaves blew across the barracks. Down in one of the boiler rooms a work gang demanded to see the commandant. In person. The guard blinked, and left to fetch him.

The commandant arrived in his sweaters and greatcoat. His nose was running. He had a headache. "What's the problem, boys? What is it?"

The coal shovelers stared at him. They were stripped to the waist. Their chests glistened with sweat. Coal dust covered their young faces. Their eyes were like ivory. One of the prisoners stepped forward. "We been working six hours like this without a break, and the prospect is four more. It's the same, day in, day out. There's scarce a chance to catch our breath. Here. It's your turn. We're taking a whistle!" He held out his shovel toward the commandant.

Outside, the wind howled.

"What's your name?" the commandant said.

"Carl Augustus Anderson. General Prisoner 60211. Life in prison for telling the registration board what they could do with their lousy war, which is now over and done with." He smiled. His teeth were white as ivory too. "You can call me Swede. I'll answer to it."

The commandant stalked from the room. In the hallway outside he passed a dozen soldiers.

Later, Swede Anderson shrugged it off. "Roughed us up a bit, not bad," he told the others. "We had the odds—one of us for every two of them. If they could fight they would have been in France, having at the Heinies. I've had worse at the hands of cops and railroad dicks. Hell, I'm for an eight-hour day, but I don't want to work all eight. I'll gladly fight! By the time they were done with us, the fire in the boiler was out again."

"What building does that boiler serve?"

"Part of the first wing, and the commandant's office. Had a lot of trouble with it lately."

"You look mighty fine in a black eye, red bird," Covelli said. "I had a few myself, here and there."

"I guess we can be friends," Swede Anderson said.

He stuck out his hand. Covelli extended his. They shook on it like regular pals. In one swift motion the Swede pulled Covelli across his knee and put him on the floor.

"We're in it together," Covelli agreed when he rose to his feet. He joined in the laughter.

The commandant sat in his cold office with his legs crossed and smoked a cigar. His aide sat likewise.

"Who is their leader," the commandant asked.

"There is no leader. They seem to be one. Slacker and soldier alike."

"They'll keep. It's up to the War Department what to do."

Back in the seventh wing Daniel stood alone at the bars of the cell door.

"It's Jake I think about," he said. "I think he's blind. His eyes don't ever close."

Daniel awoke with a start in the middle of the night. It was his night for the floor, along with Covelli and Jack Burton. For a moment he couldn't see. Then he imagined himself back in Camp Merrill on that hot prairie morning when he had awakened to find Jacob Decker towering over him.

He sat up suddenly.

The cell block was dark and cold. He heard a steady banging on the bars, as though someone was trying to get out.

"What is it?" Covelli muttered.

"Archies at three o'clock," Jack Burton said in his sleep. "Cannon straight ahead."

The banging grew louder.

"Come on, you babies! Up you go," a guard called out, close at hand. "Rise and shine, boys! Get yourselfs dressed! It's mighty cold outside! Bring them coats along, boys! Dreaming's over!"

The guard strolled past Daniel's cell, dragging a short piece of iron pipe against the bars as he went and singing out his cheerful greeting to the sleeping inmates.

It was four-thirty in the morning.

"We mean business! Up you go! Come on, you babies," the guard shouted from the end of the walkway. He clanged down the metal stairs to the tier below. Upstairs and down, other guards were doing the same. Soon more guards appeared, some still in overcoats. They threw back the bolts on the cell doors, and turned on some lights. The prisoners stumbled from their cells.

"Single file," a guard said, and moved down the row.

"What's going on?" Covelli called after him.

He received no answer.

Daniel and his cellmates slumped in single file against the cold wall in the walkway. The line inched forward. At the end of the corridor the line went around a large post and headed toward the stairs, where it was joined by prisoners from the tier above. The line moved even more slowly. Ten minutes later Daniel and the others had reached the landing one floor down.

"They're setting us free," someone called out.

"Not a chance!"

"My mother wants me!"

"Good-bye, everyone! Good-bye! Good-bye!"

"Shut up down there," a guard yelled from above.

"I wish I knew where we're going," Covelli said.

"They found a dentist. They want to check your teeth," said Swede Anderson.

"We're going to the hole," Daniel said.

Everyone grew quiet. Finally someone from the back of the line said, "All of us?"

"Too many," Jud Taylor said. He turned around and called up the stairs, "Remember that, boys! There's too many of us for the hole!" His voice was shaking.

"Single file! Eyes front! You slackers know single file?" the guard shouted back. "Let's have quiet down there!"

Sweat broke out on Daniel's forehead.

When the line reached the first floor, it stretched out the length of the seventh wing. The prisoners shuffled forward, craning their necks to see what lay ahead. Soon they could smell the cold night air. The doors at the far end of the corridor were standing open. The stone gangway leading out into the yard seemed to be filled with officers.

"What is it," Daniel asked, pushing lightly against Covelli's back.

"Can't see," Covelli said.

A moment later he added, "It's something—I don't know..."

Then he said, "You send that letter? The one to Knels Prairie?"

The line speeded up. Before Daniel could answer he was swept toward the arched gangway. The voices of the men ahead of him rose. A few started to shake.

The simple coffin sat on two wooden trestles in the center of the gangway, flanked by officers. It was too small. Jacob Decker's head bent to one side. His jaw seemed to be broken or dislocated. It too was slung to the side. Rouge covered his cheeks. His eyes were finally closed, but his lips were already pulling open. Daniel could see the gut thread that had been used to sew them crudely together. There was a thin patch of frost on Jacob's temple.

He was dressed in the uniform of the United States Army.

"Come on! Move along now! Back upstairs!"

The men hurried through the gangway and into the prison yard. The air was bitter cold. Dry snow swirled across the hard ground. Covelli stumbled along ahead of Daniel. No one spoke.

Covelli spread his arms out wide, toward the brilliant winter stars.

"Back to his people, a soldier after all," Covelli said.

"Don't dream," Jack Burton said.

Winter set in. The work gangs shoveled and washed, the guards grew lazy or were transferred, the mail was just as bad. Newspapers were passed from cell to cell, brimming with news about a world made safe for democracy. They were read with such hunger they fell apart in the inmates' hands, and then were passed page by page.

"Will we ever be free?" someone said.

"There's talk they may reduce courts-martial to peacetime terms," Jud Taylor said.

"Let us pray," Covelli added.

"I been in jails from Ashtabula to you-name-it," Swede Anderson declared. "In or out, it's much the same. But for the bars we're free. You're free inside or not at all."

"I tend to think you're wrong."

There was silence in the cell.

"I think continually of my father," Daniel said finally. "I've thought of Jake and what he stood for."

"So?"

"Everything touches everything else, don't it? One man's stand affects all. My pa knew one way trying to be free, Jake another. Covelli still a third. It brings us all together, is what it does."

"Not me," Jack Burton said. "No thanks."

"What's got into you, Daniel?" Covelli said.

"He's lonesome," someone said.

"Lonesome for liberty."

"Ain't we all? Why else did we stand?"

The snow drifted across the prison yard. It swept in graceful banks against the walls, sculpted by the wind. It glistened in the winter sun.

1919

15

The rooms above the music store proved comfortable, but not the same as the house at South Hill. In the evenings sad Germanic melodies floated through the floor from Frisco Fritz's chambers. Late at night there was often noise from Hurley's saloon and Mary Lane's. Once there was even a gun fight, which made more business for Simon Turner and a rush job for Guy Martini, the cabinetmaker. Draymen were by nature noisy. So were the mule skinners who drove their teams back and forth on the prairie between the depot and Camp Merrill.

Jamie's face had changed. His mouth was wider; his eyes had grown reflective.

"What do you find different?" Livia said one day. "Do you find it better or worse?"

"No clouds," he said. "No crickets and no meadowlarks. No peace of mind at all, cooped up here as we are. I ain't seen a genuine jackrabbit now for several years."

"You're exaggerating!"

"No fields. No sky. No wind. No prairie smells. It ain't the same. I find it better to be free," Jamie said. "We ever going back?"

"Someday, perhaps."

Frisco Fritz furnished more than bedclothes and Dresden

plates. In his messy cellar he found two bedsteads, a chair with no back, three kettles and a cast-iron skillet, a muffin tin of unusual shape, a cord rug, several illustrations of Dresden cut from magazines, a likeness of Beethoven, a souvenir scroll from the San Francisco Fair, and a sewing machine that had belonged to his late wife, Emma. Emmett Minor helped him carry it all upstairs.

"I'm good at lifting," Emmett said. "There's one thing I do well."

"There's no end to what a man may find if he turns his pockets inside out," said Frisco Fritz.

"And his heart," Livia said. "We thank you."

"I wish I was a soldier," Jamie said. "If it was me, I'd be a soldier."

From the rear window of the apartment Livia could look down upon a few frame houses on scattered lots in back of town. The front window showed the burned-out store next to Hurley's, the piles of coal along the tracks, the gaping boards and woodbins of the warehouse adjacent to the depot. The railroad engineers always sounded their steam whistles and rang their engine bells when everyone in town was fast asleep. Drifting across the open fields, they sounded lonesome or promising by turn. They spoke of distant places and sleep rounded off with gentle dreams. In town they woke everyone with a sudden start. "It's tomorrow coming through!" William Waters would declare. "We're high-ballin' towards a merry future night and day!"

"I do believe you're right, James Peter. It's not the same," Livia said. "In addition, not one of us is free so long as one still stands in jail for conscience."

She spent most of her time at the sewing machine.

"I'll spread the word, with my usual discretion," said Frisco Fritz.

Miss Mary Cole was the first to arrive.

She stood in the doorway to Livia's rooms with an armful of dresses that needed work and a canvas bag filled with fine delaine bought at Pearl City.

"What's your price," Mary asked. Her cheeks were flushed. Her ruby lips were soft and moist.

"I don't know," Livia stammered. "I never charged before."

"Two bits a piece?"

"Sounds fair. Depending on the work."

"I'll spread the word as best I can. And these here, I want nice dresses made, somewhat emphasizing the bust and derriere."

Soon draymen, single men from out of town, farmer boys who were on their own, men from Mary Lane's saloon, and railroad workers passing through began to knock on Livia's door. One day a soldier came. His pants were ripped nearly to his belt.

"I'm having to head back to camp, but not like this," he blushed. He looked about as old as Daniel.

"Take 'em off. We'll fix 'em up."

He blushed some more.

"Who sent you up here," Livia asked.

"I was told by a certain Mary Cole."

"Then you should have no hesitation in removing your trousers."

The soldier gulped and turned his back. He dropped his pants and stepped out of them. He held them behind him in his hand. While Livia sewed, he stood in his drawers facing the corner of the wall.

"You have anybody in the war," he asked.

"A son about as old as you, in Leavenworth. A husband who's passed on."

The boy was silent.

The cook stove served for heat as well as food. Emmett Minor carried cobs up twice a day, and brought Livia news of the town. Jack Hurley was no longer speaking to his wife. Bull Hadley had a letter from his daughter in Chicago, telling of her marriage. Doc Pratt cured a case of influenza north of town. Old Solomon McKenzie was feeling very poor, choked in the chest by age and other infirmities. He had fought at Bull Run and Rappahannock. He hoped for spring, and another prairie summer.

"Well, everybody's got a dream, Emmett," Livia said. "I hope he makes it."

"Do you know Bud Curtis, who walks with a limp?"

"Yes," Livia answered.

"So do I."

Neither death nor peace seemed to change the town's feelings. Frank Sacco, the barber, once hailed Livia on the street but hurried on without another word. Kate Hoover gave correct change at the market, but little else. Perhaps the time was not yet ripe. Sheriff Abel Bonner bespoke her case in and out of both saloons, but found few takers. "You don't believe that fair is fair?" he'd say. "I thought that's what we fought the war for. Why not give credit when it's due?"

Livia carried on. She paid her rent to Frisco Fritz on time each month.

There was a cold regularity to her days. Then one afternoon Doc Pratt stood in the doorway stamping snow from his boots. "I'm taking an awful chance to ask you this," he said, "but I'm heading down to Pearl City on a difficult confinement. Would you care to ride along?"

"What chance do you take?"

"That you'll say no."

"I never been in a motorcar."

"Well, come along then, Liv. Do you good."

"What will people say?"

"I couldn't guess. On top of that, I don't believe I care."

She wrapped herself in tattered coats, hand-me-downs no one wanted. When they passed the snowy lane leading up to South Hill, Livia turned her head the other way so as not to see. The motorcar rattled south down the town road.

"Your cheek's a-bloom already, Livia. Close work's not good for no one," Doc Pratt observed. He held the steering wheel with both gloved hands. He peered at the white ribbon of road over his frosted spectacles.

"Have to ride the middle or we'll fall right off."
"Is that so?"
"Do you ever hear from Daniel?"
"Indeed I do. Regular, about once a year."
He peered sideways at her. "The mail doesn't improve?"
"It's prison. We can't expect much more than what we get. I've heard twice since the war's been over, Homer. And I write him every week, not knowing whether he hears or not. I told him of South Hill and all—"
"You go on faith."
"I'm sure he hears."
"I see last week they let some go. A hundred and ten of the overtly religious."
"He wasn't one."
They rode along in silence for a while.
"I give him credit for his conscience and his courage," Doc Pratt finally said. "It's a precious thing to stand as he has done, against all."
"There's more like him. He hasn't stood alone."
Doc Pratt wasn't listening. His hands were tight on the wheel.
"And I give credit, too, to Pete, who loved that boy with all his heart. I give credit to you, Livia. I give credit where it's due. I give credit to you both for standing by him, come whatever may."
"I didn't always."
Doc Pratt stared straight ahead.
"I give no credit to myself at all," he said.
His voice was strangely thick. Livia looked at him. There were tears on his cheeks. She looked away, quickly. The sky was clean. The snow was pure and glistening white.
"It's the season for pneumonia," he said at last. "Colds and such as that."
"I sure do like a motorcar. Beats horses any day. Homer? It was very kind of you to ask."
It was the first sign of a thaw.

Spring came by surprise, melting all the hardness from the earth. Out on the prairie there were patches of indigo and ground plums. The fields were swept with gold and green. The roads dried. Each day brought more wagons and motor trucks into town. Camp Merrill was closing down. Before long, wheat waved high in the fields. Clouds boiled up from Texas, bringing heat. Larks sang. The prairies slowly yielded to oxeyes and milkweed and golden alexanders.

Carrie Curtis practiced patience and humility.

She sat on the back of a box wagon in the welcome shade of the cottonwood, swinging her legs. Thomas Riley, the hired hand, stood next to her. Beneath the brim of his straw hat his face was darkly handsome. He rolled a cigarette.

"Ever hear from that boy you were soft on?"

"Hardly ever."

He kicked at the dirt with his boot.

"Your eyes are very beautiful," he said.

"Thank you, Tom."

He scratched his ear.

"Your lips divine."

"Tom!"

He cleared his throat.

"A girl like you is quite a woman," he declared.

Carrie didn't answer. She glanced over her shoulder toward the house.

"I guess to all things there's a season," he said. "I seen some folks out to threshing."

"We start next week."

"Even men and women have their season," he said. "Want a drag?" He took the cigarette out of his mouth and held it toward her. She looked over her shoulder again. Her legs stopped swinging.

"How far would you run with me, Tom?"

He put the cigarette back between his lips. It was his turn to check the house.

"You looking to get away?"

"Just how far would you run?" she said. Her legs started to swing again.

The corners of his mouth turned down. There was a furrow in his brow. "To the ends of the earth, I suppose. At the very least to the town of Prairie Flower, where I hear they have a very fine hotel."

He gave her a sudden smile, handsome as ever. She didn't move. He edged closer. "I believe I'll steal a kiss," he said. "Don't blow the whistle on a working man." He leaned over and nibbled gently on her neck.

Carrie's gray eyes flashed, as though her heart had been ignited. She stared to the east across the fields of waving wheat.

The telegram arrived that evening. Livia was at the sewing machine. Jamie was at the front window, admiring the courier's gleaming motorcycle in the street below. The knock at the door startled them both.

"It's us!" Jamie said.

"It is indeed," the courier replied when Livia opened the door. "Mrs. Livia Hanson?"

She tore the yellow envelope with trembling fingers:

"RELEASED HOME TOMORROW DANIEL."

The courier closed the door himself.

A while later, when her tears had dried, she turned to Jamie. "Would you like to take a run down the town road, to Carrie Curtis?" She glanced past him, out the window. The rooms in which she lived seemed unsuited for the expansion of her heart. She refolded the slip of paper and handed it to Jamie.

"You'll have to hurry for the dark," she added.

The train raced westward over the plains. The light was harsh and flat. The sun stood overhead. There were no shadows. The chatter of the wheels and rails reverberated throughout the car. It grew louder now and then when the porter or a passenger walked through, grabbing wildly at the seats to keep his balance.

"We're going like sixty."

"We're going mighty fast, that's true," Daniel agreed.

"Traveling light, I see."

"Any lighter, I fear I'd float," Daniel said.

He stared out the window at Kansas. The soldier in the seat next to him had tried to start a conversation ever since the train left Leavenworth station.

"It's a God-forsaken country, ain't it now?" the boy said, peering out past Daniel at the landscape. Fields of wheat whizzed by, and county roads, and little boys at play; low-slung wires for the telegraph, and silos filled with grain.

"It ain't so bad, all in all."

"I'm from Angeles myself. City of Angels. My perception is, you either been in jail or a mighty hard storm, judging by the cut of that nice suit."

Daniel glanced at his sleeve. The suit coat was a good three inches shorter than his shirt sleeve.

"I been in both, to tell the truth. Prison and a storm."

"The old D.B. at Leavenworth?"

"You nailed it."

"Well, I'll be damned! Whatever for?"

Daniel turned and faced him. The soldier's uniform was crisp and clean. He had ribbons on his chest. His cap was cocked at a jaunty angle. "For violent opposition to the war," Daniel confided. "Trying to kill the President and several of his cabinet."

They rode in silence for miles, past Slinger and Silver Creek and on to Cornucopia, where another stop was made. Daniel watched the towns pass. Each mile brought him nearer to home and farther from the seventh wing. He and Covelli and Otis Judson Taylor had been released together, on reduced sentences. What once was life in prison was now time served. Covelli headed south to New Orleans, hoping for a seaman's berth. Jud Taylor was bound for Massachusetts. They parted like strangers, having nothing left to say. "Good-bye! Good-bye," Jud Taylor called. "Good-bye," Covelli cried. "Good-bye, boys," Daniel said. And that was all. Swede Anderson remained behind for starting a riot in the messhall and then pinching a guard's fingers in a door repeatedly. Even in peacetime assault was still punished. Jack Burton was also left behind, waiting to be interviewed by a military psychologist who was always busy elsewhere. He was a regular soldier and took it well. "Nothing's fair, after all," Burton had said. "I hoped I'd be the first one out. It just don't pay to dream."

"Leavenworth is where I mustered out," the soldier next to Daniel said at last. "I served in France at first and then Archangel, in the country of Russia. Under Brit command, of course. Withdrawn last month, New York last week, Leavenworth—and now I'm free. My name is Dennis Miller, by the way. Cornish, on my mother's side. I hope to make it big in pictures. The moving pictures. The war was a fizzle, so far as my money goes. But pictures is the coming thing, with fame and fortunes to be made. Ever consider it, a good-looking lad like you? You got anything to go home to? You even going home? You ain't really dangerous, are you? You're feeding me Bull Durham! Come on out to Hollywood!"

"Well, I got a girl I used to have. A farm, near to a place called Winchester, of which there ain't much left. I hope to start anew. My father's passed away. My mother's still alive. I got a baby brother there at home."

"Come out to Hollywood! There's room for all!"

Daniel laughed out loud. The soldier seemed startled.

"You know, that's funny," he continued. "I ain't known a single girl to wait. They're mighty indirect about it too. They say they love you. They write you pretty letters about missing you and such. They hint at all their heart's romance. But nothing turns out what it seems. It's happened to a lot of boys I know."

"I'm counting on her," Daniel said.

"My heart's been broken more than once," the soldier added.

"I know that looking at me you can't tell. I hide it very well. But it's been broke."

"I'm counting on her," Daniel said.

He turned sideways in his seat, to discourage any more conversation. Posts and fences flew by, and empty roads beneath a turquoise sky. Streamers of cloud clung to the horizon. The light was soft and white. Elam passed, then Fairwater.

"The next one's home," the soldier said behind him. "I can tell the way you watch that window."

"The next one's Prairie Flower," Daniel said. "Then comes what may."

The train began to slow. The town drifted into view: a few elevators along the tracks, some piles of stove wood and coal. There were storefronts down the street, and a grand hotel. The door flew open at the end of the car, and the conductor called out the town. Daniel watched the window: the platform sliding by, a baggage cart, a girl in white, a family with its bags and boxes, some boys in tattered clothes.

He turned and looked the soldier in the face.

"You will excuse me!" he said. He scrambled out of the seat and raced for the back of the car, flinging open the door and stepping out on the foyer. The conductor glanced back and stuck out his arm. "One moment, son! Until she stops complete!"

Daniel leaned around him, looking back. He cried out her name as loudly as he could.

She was still at the end of the platform, holding onto her hat and searching the windows of the other cars. One call was all it took. She turned and ran up the platform toward him. Her skirts flew. Her hair flew. Her eyes sparkled.

"Prair-r-rie Flower," the conductor shouted.

Daniel braced himself, but Carrie pulled up short. Her cheeks were flushed.

"I waited!" she said. "I couldn't wait!"

"I'm glad you did! You couldn't?"

She looked him up and down.

"Are you much changed?"

"Not that I noticed, that's for sure!"

"Do you still care," she asked.

"I care!" Daniel said. "Do you wonder how I knew it's you? I never seen that dress before, I never seen you wear a hat in all my life, I never seen those shoes before—"

"How? I give!"

"You got the longest neck on any girl I ever seen!"

Her eyes filled up with mock surprise. Before she could say a word, Daniel lifted her in his arms and spun her around.

"Ladies! Gentlemens!" the conductor said.

"How did you get here?" Daniel demanded, holding her tightly. Their faces were an inch apart.

"There was a fellow promised to take me to the ends of the earth," Carrie confessed. "I came this far. He went on. I told you, Daniel Hanson! You ain't the only one!"

"You're still the one for me!" He swung her in his arms and put her on the train. Then he kissed her.

The doors closed behind them.

The train began to move.

The miles flew by without a thought of war. The sun descended. It sent out waves of light. Wheat fields stretched to the horizon.

In town the light was fading. It flooded up against the buildings like the ebb tide of an era—a time, a place, a circumstance that would never come again. The bunting and the flags had all been taken down. Frank Sacco sat on a stool before his barbershop, remembering Genoa. Mae Murphy stood in the doorway to Hadley's store, shielding her eyes from the sun. She thought of glades of wood and woodcocks flying up before her feet. James Kent was on the road again with all his photographic apparatus, capturing on emulsion the great disparity between light and darkness. Langer, the bootmaker, never had come home from

Texas, even though the war was won. Where had he landed? Laredo? A ditch outside of Yuma? Matamoros? In Flanders Field? Bull Hadley had his dreams of power, and his ashtray, and his cronies. Jack Hurley kept his mouth shut. Sam Briggs had supper every night in Mary Lane's saloon, hoping to catch the eye of Mary Cole.

Evening was coming on. Livia led them up the lane through thimblegrass and bristle. The corn in the south field lay bent and broken, a harvest delayed too long. In the corner of the yard the verbena was in bloom. The house itself was nearly level to the prairie: charred timbers, cross beams, chimney bricks.

Daniel moved slowly around it.

"It's just as I imagined," he said. "But even ruin and desolation can be overcome."

"It's hard work, Daniel."

"Well, and what not?"

"It's hard, uncertain work."

"Well, here's a start.... He walked to the highest part of the prairie rise and kicked at the sod with his boot. The grass flew off, disclosing the waiting earth beneath. He turned and looked down at the others.

"I'm willing," Carrie said, coming up the rise to join him. Livia came along as well. The breeze ruffled the hem of her skirts. "I can hammer. I can hoe," she said. "I don't particularly hanker to sew, however—"

"Well, *I* can sew!" Carrie said.

"And raise up kids!" Daniel added.

They looked off over the fields, through all the vast expanse of sky and shadow. The evening seemed to rise around them and embrace them in its folds. The countryside was restful and at peace.

Halfway down the rise behind them, Jamie's eyes were calm and brown. His cheeks were lean. He held his rifle carved from wood. It pointed first at Daniel's back, and then at Livia's slender breast, and then at Carrie's pretty face as she looked back over her shoulder in surprise. And then South Hill, and then the sky. Slowly, Jamie began to spin. His arms stretched wide. His face turned upward. He turned in circles on the slanted ground, uncertain of his footing. The world began to tilt and sway, the sky became the earth, the earth became the sky, the evening stars flew by, until he fell to the earth and lay still.

He held fast to his gun.

His eyes looked bravely up to heaven.